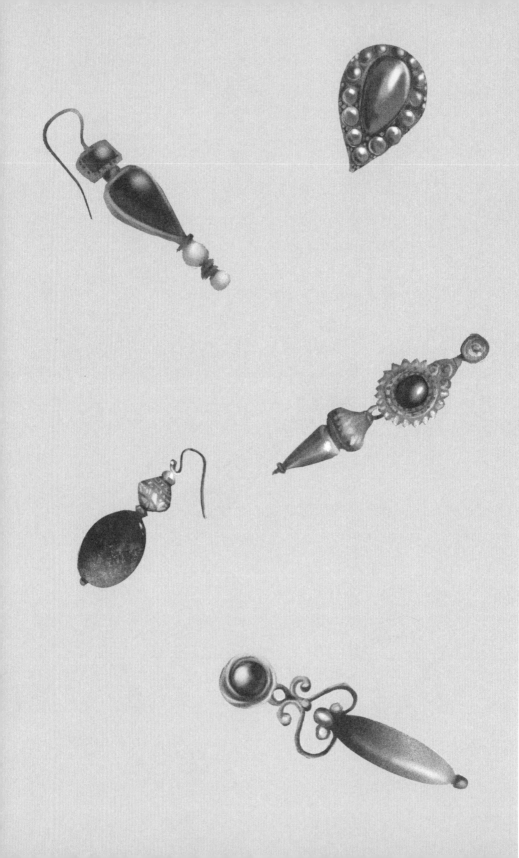

MOIRA'S PEN

MEGAN WHALEN TURNER

MOIRA'S PEN

A QUEEN'S THIEF COLLECTION

ILLUSTRATIONS BY
Deena So'Oteh

GREENWILLOW BOOKS
An Imprint of HarperCollins*Publishers*

I'm grateful to my agent, Jane Putch, and my editor, Virginia Duncan, for making this book possible; to my friend Sharyn November, for her contribution; and to Deena So'Oteh and the team at Greenwillow—especially Paul Zakris—for making it so very beautiful.

"Eddis Goes Camping" was originally published in *The King of Attolia* (2007 paperback); "Breia's Earrings" in *Disney Adventures*, August 2000; "Destruction" in *A Conspiracy of Kings* (2011 paperback); "Knife Dance" in *The Queen of Attolia* (2017 paperback); "Wineshop" in *The King of Attolia* (2017 paperback); "The River Knows" and "Envoy" in *Thick as Thieves* (2017 hardcover); and "Alyta's Missing Earrings" in *Return of the Thief* (2020 hardcover).

The text of this book is set in 12-point ITC Galliard.
Book design by Paul Zakris

Library of Congress Cataloging-in-Publication Data is available.
ISBN 9780062885609 (hardcover) |
ISBN 9780063274242 (Owl Crate ed.)
22 23 24 25 26 PC/LSCH 10 9 8 7 6 5 4 3 2 1
First Edition

GREENWILLOW BOOKS

Moira's Pen

Moira is the messenger of the gods. She carries a feather pen, sometimes in her hand, sometimes behind her ear. In the past, Moira loaned her pen to mortals. When the historian Eutritus succumbed to temptation and used it not just to record history, but to alter it, Moira promised the Great Goddess Hephestia never to do so again. After that, historians could only pray that she would guide their pens and be their muse.

Not only historians prayed to her, though. All wordwrights did. Every year a playwriting competition was held in Moira's honor in the city of Attolia. The plays were performed during the Moirian Festival, and the winner of the competition would receive a feather pen crafted from solid gold.

Nearest of the gods to mortals, Moira sees them in all their folly and their wisdom and records what she sees. When people wished for something to come true they would say, "May it be written with Moira's pen."

—*D'Aulaires' Myths of the Little Peninsula*

Table of Contents

A Conversation with the Muse ⟩⟫ xi

A Letter to Readers ⟩⟫ xii

Eddis Goes Camping ⟩⟫ 1

The Princess and the Pastry Chef ⟩⟫ 25

A Trip to Mycenae ⟩⟫ 28

Breia's Earrings ⟩⟫ 35

Fibula Pins ⟩⟫ 45

Burning Down the House of Kallicertes ⟩⟫ 47

Bee Pendant ⟩⟫ 51

The Watch Takes the Thief ⟩⟫ 52

The Lion Gate ⟩⟫ 56

The Destruction of Hamiathes's Gift ⟩⟫ 59

The Molossian Hound ⟩⟫ 66

In the Queen's Prison ⟩⟫ 68

The Games of Kings ⟩⟫ 70

Vapheio Cups ⟩⟫ 74

Knife Dance ⟩⟫ 76

Wineshop ⟩⟫ 88

Eddis's Earrings ⟩⟫ 92

The Portland Vase ❧ 94

Envoy ❧ 96

The Cook and the King of Attolia ❧ 101

Brinna's Almond Cakes ❧ 111

Ina and Eurydice Borrow a Beehive ❧ 114

Music to Delight the Ear ❧ 116

Lamassu ❧ 120

The Royal Game of Ur ❧ 122

Melheret's Earrings ❧ 124

The Arrival ❧ 129

The River Knows ❧ 131

Alyta's Missing Earring ❧ 133

News from the Palace ❧ 148

The Queen of the Night ❧ 152

Immakuk and Ennikar and the Gates of Heaven ❧ 154

The End of Eddis ❧ 166

Gitta ❧ 172

Some Persons of Significance ❧ 185

A Conversation with the Muse

What are you doing?

Writing.

Writing what?

An introduction to *Moira's Pen*.

An introduction to my pen?
Did you borrow my pen?

No. Your pen is fictional.

I am also fictional.

Yes.

But you are talking to me.

That's because I am engaging in *fiction*.

I thought you were writing an introduction.

That, too.

What does your introduction say?

How much I'd like to borrow your pen.

A Letter to Readers

When *Return of the Thief* was published, people asked me if I was sad to be finished with my series and if I would miss my characters. It was a hard question to answer. While I did finally get to the end of the story I've been telling for the last twenty-five years, I've always deliberately left space in my writing—room for my readers' imagination to work, room for my own imagination to work.

I confess that even then this book was at the back of my mind.

Many years ago, I was asked to write a short piece set in the world of The Queen's Thief for a new paperback edition of one of the books. I can't remember now if I wrote "Eddis Goes Camping" or "The Destruction of Hamiathes's Gift" first. I just know that I found the invitation a delightful excuse to abandon the narrative track and go exploring in my own world. As time passed and I continued to work on the Geniad, some of my short pieces have gone into editions that are now out of print. While I know from my own experience the joy of locating that rare copy of a favorite book, as a writer, I always want to make it easier for my readers to find what I've written.

So, *Moira's Pen* is a compendium for pieces already published and for the others that have never been published before. It's also the solution to a painful dilemma. As I was finishing *Return of the Thief*, I had two stories in mind, "Alyta's Missing Earring" and another. Only one of them could be at the end of the book, and deciding between them was killing me. Thanks to the magic of Moira's pen, the other is here.

As I gathered these pieces together, I was reminded of the way writing each of them inspired more worldbuilding that, in turn, yielded inspiration for the future. If I had Moira's pen in my hand right now, I could write a whole book explaining exactly how inspiration works, but I do not and cannot. Instead, I've encouraged someone who is both invention *and* inspiration to add some comments of her own. I might not be able to write with Moira's pen, but she can.

To my readers, I mean it when I say that I have been honored by your attention. I am, as ever, gratefully yours,

Megan Whalen Turner

Megan Whalen Turner

"Do not offend the gods."

MOIRA'S
PEN

Helen thought she found the temple on her own. She woke without the warmth of her fire, unaware that she was both Ending and Beginning.

Eddis Goes Camping

The pony was fat and shaggy still from the winter. Its short legs flicked across the hard-packed road and Helen's own round, solid body bounced uncomfortably on its back. She had a bundle with her, but it was as small as she could make it, just blankets, a loaf of bread, and other bare necessities. She had her belt knife, and her own crossbow hung on the saddle with the cranking mechanism geared for her nine-year-old arms. With luck, anyone who noticed her riding up the road away from the palace would see nothing out of the ordinary and would forget her again quickly.

The Spring Festival was finally over and everyone was in bed recovering. Helen doubted that anyone but Xanthe, her nurse, would even wonder where she was. By bedtime, of course, Xanthe would be alarmed, but by bedtime she would have found the drawing chalked inside the door to Helen's sleeping room. Xanthe couldn't read, or Helen would have written a note. Instead, she had drawn a picture of her pony with its bundle of blankets and food, and a picture of herself waving good-bye.

It was only for one night, and Xanthe would eventually forgive her, but only if Helen made it away from the palace without drawing anyone's attention. If her mother sent for her and Helen couldn't be found, people would assume she was playing with her cousins in some obscure part of the palace . . . so long as no busybody remembered that she had gone out on her pony. If that happened, his stall would be checked, and when it was found empty, the hue and cry would be frightful. Her aunts would start wailing that she and the horse had gone over a cliff or been eaten by a lion, and her father would send out the entire population of the capital city in a search. At the thought, Helen urged the pony on a little faster.

Finally, their path left the Sacred Way. It cut across the shoulder of the hill and then down to the valley road that led up into the hunting preserves. Out of sight of the palace, once among the trees, Helen relaxed. The pony slowed, and she patted his neck.

"Don't slow too much, Nestor," she told him. "We have a long way to go." The place she was heading for was more than half a day's ride away. She'd found it the previous fall when she wandered much farther than she'd intended. There had only been time for a quick look and a promise to return after the winter was over.

She had been out before on overnight hunting expeditions, and she'd sometimes spent whole days out on her own. This wouldn't be very different, and it was the only way she could explore her secret hideaway and still keep it secret.

The secrecy was essential, because without it the place wouldn't be hers alone. At the very least, she would have to share it with other children her age, but it was more likely that someone older, one of the new spears, would take it and chase the children away. Someone like her brother Pylaster, who had just left the boys' house and received his first spear, would declare it his personal kingdom, and only his closest friends would be allowed to join him there. He would lose interest eventually, when he wasn't a new spear anymore, but by then some other new spear would have claimed it. Helen would never have a chance.

By the time she reached the age when a boy received his spear, she would have left sword practice and horseplay behind and undergone the mysterious alteration that would make her a young woman with long skirts and jewels in her ears and no interest in anything sensible. She rolled her shoulders in distaste at the thought, but she had seen it happen to too many cousins to doubt its inevitability. Her mother must have her way. For the time being, however, there was freedom, exercised with discretion.

Helen arrived in the early afternoon. The day was gray and the spring wind was chilly. High up in the mountains there was still quite a bit of snow, and she shivered even in her sheepskin jacket. She wished the sun were shining. The narrow valley was dark and much less inviting than she'd anticipated. The temple itself, when she reached it, was desolate, the marble cold and gray and lifeless. She hesitated a moment before she swung down from Nestor's back. He was nervous and jerked at the reins as she tied them to a sapling.

He whickered, as if to say there was still time to make it back home before dark. "Don't be silly," she said aloud. She'd been looking forward to the trip all winter and she wouldn't quit, even though the high sides of the valley made her feel very small. She started for the temple with the stubbornness that so often drove Xanthe to despair.

The temple must have been impressive once. Sitting sideways across the end of the narrow valley, its entrance porch at one end facing and nearly brushing the cliff face before it, it was as large as any temple Helen had ever seen. Its pillars and interior walls still stood, though most of its roof was gone. Rubble had fallen from the cliff face, burying the approach to the front entryway, but the temple's foundation was stepped on all sides, so it was easy for Helen to climb up to the terrace and slip between the pillars. Holes in the walls made it unnecessary to go through the front doors. Helen crawled across the tops of fallen stones nearly as high as her waist and slipped into the naos.

The floor was a dangerous wash of broken roof tiles mixed with the remains of the timbers that had supported them. The marble walls were bare. The statuary of the friezes had come down and smashed; lighter chunks of white marble were mixed with the roofing. Beside Helen was a piece from the head of a horse, and next to it was a broken-off hand with a bit of marble rein still running through it. The statue must have been beautiful when it was whole, and Helen was flooded by a sudden sadness. If Nestor had whickered again, she would have gone home.

He didn't, so she squared her small but sturdy shoulders and picked her way to a hole in the far wall. Halfway across, she paused to look toward the bare stone altar. The roof above was intact and the marble floor under it was mostly clear, but the pedestal that had once held a statue of some god or goddess was empty.

On the far side of the naos, there was a larger hole in the wall and an open path between the fallen stones. Once she was clear of the rubble and had a look at what lay before her, she stopped. She was so pleased that she hugged herself. The terrace on the far side of the temple was mostly free of broken masonry, and beyond it was an outdoor room, with the steep cliffs at the end of the valley for walls. The grass there was already green with the advance of spring. Under the gray skies, it seemed to glow with its own light. There were paths laid out, and the hedges of a garden, still visible, at one side. But mostly there was just the smooth carpet of the grass, and beyond it the opening of a cave in the cliffs.

The cave was a potential problem. Helen eyed it carefully for several minutes, then she went back for Nestor. It wasn't easy to coerce him up the stepped foundation and across the terrace behind the back of the temple, but once he reached the grassy carpet, he seemed happy enough, and she relaxed. The sun had started to break through the clouds, the sacred space behind the temple had begun to seem almost welcoming, and Nestor wouldn't have dedicated himself to the grass with such an appetite if he'd smelled a mountain lion's lair in the nearby cave.

She pulled off his bridle and left him to graze while she explored. The longer she stayed, the more at home she felt. Something very tight in her chest seemed to release itself, slowly unwinding, like thread off a spindle. On reflection, she decided the metaphor might not be apt. "I'd be in a mess the way Agape's yarn always is," she murmured to herself.

She looked into the cave first, which was high but shallow. There was a darker space at the back that led deeper into the mountain, but it was a crevice too narrow even for a child. A trickle of water came out of it and flowed in a channel to a basin cut in the rock. She had a drink and filled her waterskin before she whistled for Nestor to come have a drink as well. The water was cold and tasted of snow.

When the pigeons came home in the evening, she loaded her crossbow and shot quarrels at them until it was too dark to see where they fell. She did not hit a single bird. She had brought only the loaf of bread and a packet of sugared nuts for her dinner. Sighing, she went to gather wood for the fire. The dark was rising quickly and her skin prickled with cold. She collected a stack far larger than she would need.

She started her fire on the terrace looking out over her little territory, and rolled out her blankets beside it. Opening the bag holding her food, she looked into it dubiously. Glancing over one shoulder at a hole nearby leading into the naos of the temple, she considered how much the success of her return depended on luck. With much reluctance, she then tore the loaf in half and carried one half, and all the nuts, into the temple to lay them on the altar in front of the empty plinth. Better safe than sorry.

When she had eaten the remaining half of the loaf, she rolled herself in her blankets and lay down between the fire and her woodpile to sleep. Without waking fully, she could lift the sticks from the pile and add them to the fire. She listened to Nestor snuffling as he settled down for the night, then, without knowing exactly which moment it happened, she drifted off.

The cold woke her. The cold, and the feel of the empty marble under her hand as it searched for her woodpile. Thinking she must have used up all the wood closest to her, she extended her reach. Still no wood. Sighing with frustration, she opened her eyes to the dying firelight. Her woodpile wasn't there. She sat up, still half-asleep, and looked more carefully around the terrace. There was no wood. She looked back at the fire, which was a mistake. It made her night-blind, and once she had assured herself that the little campfire could not have burned through all her wood without leaving more ash, and that she hadn't mistakenly fed it all her fuel while asleep, she was left unable to see anything else.

She turned away from the fire and waited patiently for the blindness to clear, only to see at last that every stick of her wood was gone. She almost turned to check the fire again, but Helen didn't make the same mistakes twice. She looked elsewhere instead. Before she fully realized what she was searching for, she saw it: the glow of another fire burning nearby. Burning with her wood.

Her mouth firmed and her expression hardened. Brigands wouldn't have left her sleeping, and a decent person wouldn't have taken all of the wood, even if he'd had no time to gather his own. A decent person probably would just have joined Helen at her fire. Only a sneak would take all of her wood and leave her in the cold. The list of possible suspects was long enough. Any one of the new spears would have done it. They were so full of their own importance once they were out of the boys' house. One of her cousins, or perhaps Pylaster. The bread and nuts on the altar had been an unsuccessful sacrifice. Whoever had taken her firewood was going to announce her escapade to the palace, and there was going to be a tremendous din when she got home.

The cold shuddered through her, and she clenched her fists in frustration. She wanted to take their horses and leave the arrogant new spears to walk home, but she couldn't get Nestor across the terrace without waking anyone asleep inside the temple, and she wouldn't leave him behind. She would have liked to steal the wood back but doubted she could, and even if she were successful, the older boys would wake when they felt the cold, just as she had. There wouldn't be any secrecy the next time they took it. She might be very sturdy for a girl, but she was still only nine, and tiny compared to her brother's companions. However, she was determined not to creep up like a penitent to their fire. At least she could steal back enough wood so that she could sleep the rest of the night in the warmth generated by her own fuel.

She kicked off her blankets and got quietly to her feet. The firelight was definitely coming from inside the temple, which she felt was scandalous. One shouldn't camp inside a temple, even an abandoned one. Softly, she crept along the wall toward the light. She felt carefully for fallen blocks of stone but didn't encounter any. When she reached the hole in the temple wall, she found it more door shaped than she remembered, but the regular shape of the doorway was the least of the mysteries. She crouched in the darkness, just beyond the reach of the light from the fire burning before the altar, and stared. Whoever had stolen her wood, it wasn't a new spear.

She could see through the doorway and between the heavy interior pillars that held up the roof. The marble floor was clear of debris and scattered with carpets. Standing candelabras with fine wax candles augmented the light of the fire, which burned inside the repaired walls of the fire pit. Not only was the fire pit repaired, Helen realized, but the roof and the walls. The murals were restored, and so were the friezes above them. She laid a hand on the smooth-worked masonry of the doorway, then looked back to the interior.

Bathed in the light of the fire, a woman more beautiful even than Helen's mother lay on a couch with a little table beside her, and on it a bowl filled with pigeon eggs. As Helen watched, the woman selected an egg and cracked it on the edge of the table. The larger pieces of shell she tossed toward the fire, but the smaller pieces she carelessly let fall. When they landed on the pure white cloth of her gown, she brushed them to the floor.

Looking down at her from the altar was a young man. Helen thought at first that he might be the age of a new spear, but then he looked older and she wasn't certain. He was dressed all in gray, sitting cross-legged and eating nuts out of a silver bowl. Her nuts, Helen realized. She must have made a sound. The woman on the couch shifted a little and spoke to the figure on the altar. "Who is it?"

The young man looked over at Helen, and she pulled back into the darkness.

"It's Eddis," said the man, and Helen snapped her head around in surprise, looking up and down the terrace for her father.

"She's found her firewood missing," the man continued, inexplicably. Helen could see no one else on the terrace.

"You are eating her nuts," the woman on the couch said languidly. "It was unkind to take her fire as well."

"Nonsense," he responded. "If you think I am unkind, ask her to join us."

"I suppose we can make her forget again by morning." The woman beckoned Helen with one beautiful white hand. "Do come, dear," she said.

Against her better judgment, Helen stepped cautiously as far as the interior pillars.

"The last Eddis, is it?" the goddess asked, but she was speaking to the man. "Have I seen her before? She looks like her father."

"Have you seen her father?" the young man asked, amused.

"I'm not sure. Perhaps her grandfather. Certainly she is not a pretty girl, but I suppose that is neither here nor there with this one. What's your name, dear?"

"Helen," she whispered, too bewildered to be hurt by the casual condemnation of her looks. She might not have been hurt anyway; she knew she wasn't pretty and wasn't particularly bothered. She wondered if all this was a dream. A chill breeze from the open doorway behind her swept across the back of her neck and she shivered. It felt real.

"You're cold. Come closer to the fire."

Helen took another few hesitant steps. All of her wood was in the fire pit, and she could already feel its warmth. She saw that there was a third figure watching her from the base of the altar—another woman resting against a cushion. Beside her was a lap desk, as if she had just set it aside. She still held a white quill pen in her hand as she leaned forward to look at Helen.

Another shudder went through Helen, as if someone had walked over her future grave. She waited for it to pass, but it only grew worse until she dropped to a crouch, wrapping her arms around her knees and holding tight as she stared at the woman by the altar.

"Poor chick," the woman on the couch murmured, and Helen felt a breath of warm air caress the back of her neck. The shudder faded away and in its absence came a dreamlike feeling. The woman with the white quill pen was Moira, who recorded men's fates. She was the messenger of the gods. Sitting on the altar above her, so indecently comfortable in such a sacrilegious place, was Eugenides, the Thief. Helen didn't know who the third immortal was. The goddess of the temple, she assumed. A moment before, everything had been more frightening than she could bear. Now she accepted it with less excitement than she'd felt at the loss of her firewood.

"She isn't Eddis yet," Moira pointed out calmly. "No, not yet," agreed the goddess on the couch. "But her Thief was just born, wasn't he? Yesterday? Last week?"

Moira laid down her pen, and unrolled the scroll on her lap desk. "Four years ago," she said dryly.

Her Thief? Helen wondered. There was a Thief at the Palace of Eddis, but he was old. He'd certainly been born more than four years before. He had a grandson, though, who was about that age. She remembered that the palace had been in an uproar after his birth, when he was named Eugenides after his grandfather and after the immortal who sat eating Helen's sugared nuts as if each one were a prize.

She looked up, and the Patron of Thieves smiled down at her. Such a wicked smile, Helen thought. Full of mischief and self-satisfaction and humor. He smiled like one of her grown-up cousins, Lycos, who had been exiled when Helen was six. She remembered him well; he could make you laugh one day and cry the next. When he left the court, she'd been heartbroken, and also relieved. She eyed Eugenides warily, but she had a generous nature. It tipped the balance in his favor, and she smiled shyly back at him. His own smile deepened in response, a nicer expression altogether, and Helen decided that she liked him very much, as if approval or disapproval of a god were an everyday affair.

"Have a seat here by me," said the goddess from across the fire, pointing to a cushion in front of her couch. Helen circled the fire and sat. From there, she could still see Moira, and also a heap of fabric that lay in a bundled pile beside the fire pit. Woven with different colors and kinds of thread, it was lumpy and soft in places and smooth and tight in others. Brightly colored and streaked through with dull browns and blacks, it still seemed to carry a coordinated pattern. Helen stared, trying to make it out, but too much cloth was hidden in rumples and folds.

Moira looked up from what she was writing on her lap desk. "Eugenides has stolen the fabric from the loom of the Fates. Little will happen in the world of men until they restring their loom."

"It was very bad, Gen," said the goddess over Helen's shoulder. "Everyone will be angry."

"You said you missed Moira."

"I did, didn't I? I suppose they will be angry at me, too. Such a bore. Are the pigeons roasted, Moira dear?"

The recorder looked with narrowed eyes at a row of birds

on skewers that leaned over the fire pit. "Not yet," she said.

"You aren't angry, are you, Moira?" the Thief asked in winning tones.

"No," said Moira. "You very nicely brought the weaving here, so I can catch up on my work while we visit."

"Moira is my daughter," said the goddess, behind Helen. "And we haven't seen each other for years. No, don't look it up, Moira; I don't need to know exactly how long. It is too long. You should tell those women to keep their own records."

Moira shook her head.

"Or the men. Tell the mortals to keep their own histories."

Moira smiled. "They do so much already. There is less and less work for me all the time."

"Good," said the goddess, her mother, who Helen realized must be the wind Periphys.

"I'm sure there will always be enough to keep you busy," said Eugenides. He had lain down on his stomach and had his chin propped in his hands. His knees were bent and his feet moved idly in the air.

"Busy enough," agreed Moira.

"I'd like some wine, I think," said the goddess. "Will you fetch me a cup, chickie?" When Helen looked over her shoulder, the goddess gestured to a table she hadn't seen before. She blinked, unsure if it had been there before the goddess gestured. It was in the dim light beyond the candelabras and she might have overlooked it. It was a low table with a silver inlaid top, covered with dishes of food and cups that matched the wine set. Helen got up and went to pour the wine into the mixing bowl. She carefully avoided looking at the food while she added water to the wine and swirled the two until they mixed, then turned to lift the bowl toward the altar.

She hesitated then, just for a moment; the wine sloshed in the bowl, but she steadied it without mishap. She had lifted the wine automatically for the blessing, but there was no impersonal statue of a god or goddess above the altar, just Eugenides looking sardonic. Helen considered turning to the goddess reclining on the couch, but she wasn't certain that this temple belonged to Periphys. It was unlikely that it belonged to Moira. Helen couldn't put it past Eugenides to make himself and his friends comfortable in someone else's temple. Amused, Eugenides resolved Helen's dilemma by waving one hand in benediction. The wine was officially blessed. Politely hiding her own amusement, she offered her reverence in his direction and turned back to the table to pour the mixed wine into a cup, careful not to spill a single drop. She then carried the wine to the couch and dropped to her knees, her eyes modestly lowered.

Instead of taking the wine, the goddess lifted a hand to brush Helen's cheek. She tucked a finger under Helen's chin and lifted it and looked into Helen's eyes. For a moment,

Helen saw something beyond this slightly silly woman, something so vast that Helen felt as if she were staring up into the night sky and in danger of falling into it. "She will do," she heard the goddess say. "She will do very well."

"Of course she will," said Eugenides, dropping from the altar and stepping around the rumpled pile of the Fates' tapestry. "But what she wants just now is a pigeon, so take that wine cup or I will."

Periphys reached for the cup and directed Helen back to the cushion with a smile. "Are they done?" she asked.

"Well, I am tired of waiting, so I say they are," said Eugenides. He lifted two skewers away from the fire and carried them over. To Helen's surprise, he came to her first. He squatted down in front of her to look her in the eye a moment, as if he understood the growing distress that bubbled just beneath this odd sense of comfort that Periphys had provided. How could she be Eddis? Her father was Eddis. If Helen ever did inherit the throne, she would be Eddia, the feminine version of the state name, not Eddis. And that could only happen if her older brothers Pylaster and Lias died, and probably her younger brother Janus as well. A woman could inherit the throne of Eddis, but only as a last resort. Helen might hold Pylaster in contempt most of the time, but she loved him, and Lias and Janus as well.

"Don't worry, little one, about what is to come," said Eugenides. "You will wake in the morning and all this will be a dream, gone before the dew leaves the grass. Now, eat your pigeon, which you don't deserve because you are a woeful shot. I will exchange with you for a pile of firewood and a handful of almonds." He handed her a skewer and waited until she took the first bite before he moved to Periphys. The goddess was offended at the wait, but the Thief returned her disaffected look with one of his own that left her flustered and defensive. She took the pigeon from him and turned a cold shoulder. He laughed and returned to the fire for two more pigeons, one of which he handed to Moira before he vaulted back onto the marble pedestal to eat his own.

It was quiet while they ate. Periphys sulked and picked at her food. But when she snuck a look over her shoulder at the Thief, he smiled. "You are dreadful," she told him.

Eugenides' smile only grew. Periphys sighed and rolled her eyes. Helen had a feeling that this had happened many times before. Sooner or later, the Thief was always forgiven. They talked then, Moira and Periphys and Eugenides, and like a child at any grown-up conversation, Helen understood less and less until she lost interest and concentrated on the pigeon.

She woke in the morning from her dream of gods and temples, lying on the terrace, wrapped in her blanket. The fire beside her was dead and she was stiff with cold. Shivering, she sat up. She looked first toward the empty space where her woodpile would have been and caught at the dream just as it was fading. There had been gods in the temple, she remembered, and the God of Thieves had eaten her almonds. Still shivering, she unwrapped her blanket and hurried between the fallen stones of the temple walls to the opening near the altar. The opening was a ragged hole nearly blocked by rubble, as it had been the day before. Inside the wall and the interior row of columns, the floor was again scattered with tiles and debris. The frescoes were gone and the fire pit was broken on one side. The dream seemed less real with each passing moment, but Helen clung to it as stubbornly as she had ever held on to anything in her life. On the far side of the fire pit, she dropped to her knees and swept her hands across the floor. In the cracks between the stones, there were eggshells. No large pieces, but small ones that might have fallen from the goddess's skirts.

Helen looked up at what remained of the roof over her head. In the rafters and in the niches of the metopes were a thousand pigeon nests. Of course there were eggshells between the stones. She rose and stepped quickly away from the fire pit, past where the table laden with food had stood, and dropped to her knees again. On the dirty floor, among the debris, she found what she was seeking. A splatter of wax. Fresh and clean and white, it could only have fallen from the candelabras the night before. She used her belt knife to scrape up one perfectly round wax disc and pinched it between her finger and thumb. Her thumb fitting into the depression that had formed as it cooled, she rubbed the wax thoughtfully against her finger. Then she opened her heavy sheepskin jacket and slid the disc, just the size and shape of a button, wholly unremarkable in itself, into the small purse attached to her belt. She stood to look around the temple once again. There was no other sign that the events she remembered were anything but a dream.

She slipped a finger into the purse to nudge the small bit of wax. Determined not to forget what little she still remembered, she went to fetch her pony. Nestor was uncommonly uncooperative, jerking his head and sidling away from her at every opportunity. Finally, she lost her temper and stamped her foot on the green grass carpet outside the temple. "I am not going to forget!" she said. "And I don't care how distracting you are." Almost as if he were embarrassed, the pony lowered his head and meekly approached.

On her ride home, she was drenched by a sudden shower, Nestor slid on a rocky part of the trail and almost went down, the wind blew particularly lovely white clouds across the sky, and a rainbow appeared as well. There were mysterious rustlings in the bushes and quite a few animals emerged to watch her curiously. Stubbornly, she ignored the distractions and instead went over and over what details she could remember from her dream: Lias and Pylaster and Janus dead, herself the last ruler of Eddis, the four-year-old boy who would be her Thief. From time to time, she slipped a finger into her belt purse to poke at the wax button and reaffirm her memories.

As she approached her home, worry curled up like smoke around her. If her mother had asked for her, if someone had noticed the missing pony, if Xanthe had panicked and revealed the message Helen had left . . . the possibilities infused every thought, until even the dream seemed less important than the coming moment of truth when she arrived at the entrance gate to the stableyard.

"Your Highness!" The stable master came himself to take Nestor's reins in hand. "Our royal Queen, your mother, was most concerned"—Helen's fists tightened on the reins in alarm—"that you would be back late from this morning's ride." Of course he had noticed the empty stall, and one of the stablers must have seen her bundle, but no one had given away her secret. Stony faced, the stable master said, "I assured her that I would send you to her when you returned."

"Th–thank you, cousin," she said, signaling her awareness of her debt to him with the familial address. She turned to go, but the stable master stopped her with a touch on her arm.

"If Your Highness had left a message to say where you were riding, I could have sent a messenger out. In the future, it would be a courtesy."

"Yes, of course," stammered Helen, happy to accept the

bargain. He was willing to keep her secrets in the future, but only if he knew she was safe. She could go back. Automatically, she was searching in her belt purse as she hurried across the stableyard in response to her mother's summons. She could go back. The belt purse was empty.

She hesitated, looking at her empty hand. Go back? She considered again. It had been good to camp on her own in the mountain valley, but there were other places to explore, and it had been cold there, she remembered. The narrow valley held the winter chill. She would try someplace lower in the mountains next time. There was something else that she wanted to remember, but she couldn't think what. She hurried on across the stableyard, hoping it would come to her later.

She didn't remember. Not when she played with her cousin Eugenides, by far her favorite among all her many cousins, not even when the sickness came that took all three of her brothers in a matter of days. She never returned to the narrow valley high in the hunting preserves and never visited its abandoned temple again, though she continued her independent trips, skillfully maintaining a pretense of obedience to her mother's will with the complicity of Xanthe and the stable master and an ever-growing community of supporters.

She never thought of her dream again, until the morning she woke to find a wax button on the pillow by her head.

Though it was as clean as if it had just dropped from an unregulated candle the night before, the wax hadn't soaked into the linen. It lay lightly on the cloth, and when she lifted it up, she could see the ridge she remembered, where her belt knife had scraped it free years before. When Xanthe came to the door, her cheeks wet with tears, Helen already knew that her father was dead.

"My Queen," said Xanthe, "you are Eddia."

Helen shook her head, still sorting through her newly returned memories. Knowing the consternation it would cause, and knowing she would overcome it, she said, "No, I am Eddis. The gods have told me so."

Poor chick of a foolish mother. Closely caged,
Irene will free herself someday, but not without
the help of others.

The Princess and the Pastry Chef

No one who works in the kitchens sleeps late, and the bakers rise earliest of all. That's how Brinna came to see the princess Irene slipping out of the palace, past the open doorway of the kitchen, quiet as a mouse. How she could have snuck away from her nurse, Brinna had no idea.

"Maybe she's meeting her lover," joked Emix and recoiled when Brinna backhanded him hard enough to wipe the smirk off his face.

"She's a child," Brinna reminded him. She had been shifting full-size sacks of flour in her father's bakery since she herself was a child, and Emix would watch his tongue around her in the future. Brinna hated the sly gossip in the palace. She'd been proud to win her place in the royal kitchens, and it was an honor to cook for the king, but she didn't think much of his court full of backstabbing, meanness, and rumormongering. Every day there was a new story making the rounds about this scandal or that one.

Brinna thought of her own little girl, left behind to be raised by grandparents. Brinna missed her daughter fiercely but wouldn't have her in the sculleries scrubbing pots day in and day out, soaking in the palace atmosphere like a sponge.

She set Emix enough tasks to keep him busy until dawn, then wiped her hands on her apron and followed Irene outside. The princess shouldn't be out in the dark alone. There were guards on the palace walls, but they were watching for trespassers, thieves, assassins. They wouldn't be looking out for a little girl. And what mischief was she getting into anyway, slipping away while her nurse slept? Soft footed, Brinna went to see.

Irene was climbing into the trees and swinging from the branches, an activity both perfectly ordinary and, Brinna suspected, absolutely forbidden during the day. Brinna watched silently, maternal instincts at war with circumspection. A naughty child should be marched back to her bed with a lecture along the way and nothing more to be said in the morning. That wasn't what would happen to the princess.

She would be disgraced, lose every familiar face in her apartments, and be the subject of catty comments for the rest of her life because she wanted to run with her hands outstretched between the rows of orange trees. Because she was the daughter of a woman the court despised.

Brinna hesitated until Irene approached the beehives.

Brinna almost called her away but stopped herself in time. The bees were probably sleeping, but the guards on the walls around the garden wouldn't be. Pursing her lips, Brinna crossed the garden. As she drew near to Irene, she could see a single bee in the bright moonlight, zigzagging up to the girl's open hand.

"Careful," warned Brinna, in a voice she hoped wouldn't carry too far. "Be very still."

Irene smiled at her, as unconcerned by Brinna's presence as the bee's. "She won't sting me. My mother is queen and she says queens respect one another."

"That may be, but you aren't a queen, you are a princess who should be in bed," said Brinna sternly, and was relieved to see the girl's shoulders droop, just a little, like any child in trouble.

"Off you go," she said more lightly. "And don't let me catch you sneaking away from your nurse again," she added as the little girl trotted back toward the palace. She lifted her own hand as the princess turned to wave before she disappeared inside.

After that night, whenever Brinna heard trumpets blow the change of watch, the burbling golden call that might wake any child from a sound sleep, she ordered a screen moved across the kitchen doorway. She said it was to block the draft that might interfere with the dough rising.

⟫· A TRIP TO MYCENAE ·⟪

The inspiration for the underwater temple in The Thief
is actually a cistern at the ancient city of Mycenae in Greece.

In 1992 I went to Greece for the first time. Back then they
had a sign up at the entrance to every archeological site
threatening *dire* consequences if you so much as picked the
flowers, but otherwise, they pretty much let you explore on
your own. I loved it, even though there wasn't much information provided and many things you had to figure out for
yourself. The best you could hope for were these little square
signs like glorified tent pegs scattered around a site with
numbers on them. The numbers corresponded to entries in
the Michelin Green Guide and if you didn't have a Green
Guide, too bad. Fortunately, I did have one and still have it.
I take it with me whenever I go back to Greece.

If there was very little signage, there were also very few
restrictions. When we took the ferry to the island of Delos,
which is one vast archeological site, they dropped us off on a
little dock, said to be sure not to miss the last ferry back to
Mykonos, and then they motored away. My husband and I
spent the entire day wandering all over the island—stepping
carefully through ruined buildings, looking at the mosaic

floors, standing under the massive stones propped against one another to make the roof of a shrine. If we'd been in the US there would have been a boardwalk, lined with fences, and we wouldn't have been allowed to touch anything, and everything I most wanted to see would be miles from the path, because that's what always happens to me.

If the Department of Antiquities wasn't interested in keeping tourists cooped up behind fences, it wasn't much interested in keeping them safe, either. It's not always clear in pictures, but the Parthenon, for example, on top of Athens's Acropolis, is at the edge of a perpendicular drop. This drop is marked with a line of those ankle-high tent peg signs, this time connected by the low swags of a rope, really more likely to trip you and help you over the edge than anything else. I got the impression that if you were dumb enough to fall off the Acropolis, the Department of Antiquities didn't care so long as you didn't break an Antiquity when you landed.

That is why when we were standing outside the entrance to an underground cistern several thousand years old, dressed in our tourist uniform of khaki camp shorts, white T-shirts, and hiking boots, we were stupidly considering taking the stairs down into the dark. We were in Mycenae, the most powerful city in the Peloponnese during the days of Helen of Troy. The day before we'd been in Corinth and we'd taken another inviting set of stairs into the remains of a Roman cistern, a gloriously huge room with an arched ceiling held up by rows and rows of pillars, lit by the sun's rays puncturing its broken roof, shining on the rubble underneath. It had been perfectly safe, I'm sure.

Now we were eyeing a narrower stone tunnel that turned as it descended and disappeared under a low lintel. This cistern was one of the things that had made Mycenae great back when Agamemnon was king. Fed by a spring, the Perseia, and accessible from inside the city walls, it allowed the Mycenae to hold out against any besieging neighbors.

In the United States there would have been a sign that said, "UNSAFE. KEEP BACK." In Greece, there was just an entry in the Michelin Green Guide that said, "On the left is an entrance to an underground stair; its 99 steps bend round beneath the walls to a secret cistern 18m–59ft below." What we wanted to know was whether the Perseia, after two thousand years, was still flowing.

The entryway was made of huge stones forming a narrow tunnel with a steeply pointed ceiling. It looked pretty sturdy, and I pointed out that I had a flashlight to deal with the dark. It was one of those penlights that a doctor uses to look in your eyes. My uncle had given it to me and I'd packed it for the trip feeling it might be useful. This was 1992, of course. We aren't talking about an LED.

Off we went down the stairs. They turned just before the low doorway and turned again right after it and that's when I discovered that those little pen-shaped things that the doctor uses to look in your eyes aren't really useful at all in the pitch dark. At which point, sensible people would have turned back. The stairs were decaying into a long slide of rubble. The walls around us weren't dressed stone any-more—they were the same shape, but the tunnel was carved out of solid rock, just wide enough for two people to stand side by side with their arms locked around each other, the walls sagging toward each other to meet like a narrow tent over our heads.

Without the flashlight it was literally so dark you couldn't see your hand in front of your face. I know, because I held my hand in front of my face. With the flashlight, we had just enough light to see the stair under our feet and the next one down, so we kept going, arm in arm, me holding the flashlight at chest height and pointing straight down, one slow step at a time until I asked, "Have you been counting the stairs?"

Neither of us had been counting the steps and anyway it was sort of hard to know what constituted a stair when they were in such bad shape. I wondered how the Green Guide could possibly have known there were ninety-nine. We had no idea how much farther it was to the bottom of a cistern that may or not have been filled with water, and common sense finally reasserted itself. We picked up a rock and threw it into the dark. It went thud and not plop and we had our answer, no water in Mycenae, and we turned back. We had to go just as carefully up the steps, staring at the ground in the very dim light. We'd made it around the first turn and were squeezing through the low doorway when the loudest and most prolonged real-life scream I have ever heard ricocheted against the stone walls all around us.

We were in our tourist uniforms—white T-shirts, light-colored shorts. I was holding a dim flashlight in front of me, but pointed at the stairs beneath us. It illuminated us only from the neck down. As far as the German tourist at the top of the stairs could tell, there were two headless ghostly figures coming out of the dark—it's no wonder she screamed. For one heart-stopping moment, I thought the walls might be collapsing, and then she said, "Oh, sorry!" and we all laughed. Later, she and her husband gave us a ride back to our hotel.

I wrote all about it in my travel journal that night and for obvious reasons (stupidity + terror) it stuck in my mind. Two years later, when I was writing *The Thief*, I got the journal back out, reread the details, and used them as the inspiration for the temple under the Aracthus River.

"I am a master of foolhardy plans."

For Thieves, every leap is a leap of faith. They know that Eugenides is a dangerous god to serve.

Breia's Earrings

The corridor was long, and it was a good place to pick up speed, but the stone floor was covered in rugs, and a rumple at this point could be fatal. Gen kept a careful eye on the ground in front of him and only glanced up quickly to be sure the way ahead of him was clear. Gods forbid he should run into another aunt. He had slipped by Aunt Livia only because she had been startled. Most of his aunts would have thought it beneath their dignity to clutch at a passing nephew, but not Aunt Livia. She had only missed his collar by a fingertip.

He was approaching a smaller rug. It lay like a trap in the middle of the floor, and he lifted his feet to sail over it. Behind him, he could hear the pounding footsteps of his cousins. The corridor was a good place for them to pick up speed as well, and he rather hoped that one of them might slip on the carpet. There was a stutter in the steady thump of boots. Someone may have slipped, but Gen couldn't take the time to check, and it didn't seem to have slowed the group. They were all older than he was by several years, their legs were longer, and they were gaining ground fast, yelling threats as they came. What they threatened, he couldn't quite hear, as too many voices were mingled together, but he could imagine.

What they had in mind didn't matter, though, because just ahead of him was a light well where sunshine from the skylights above fell four floors to the rooms below. His path was blocked by the railings that surrounded the open space. Already he could hear his cousins' footsteps shortening as they slowed to see which way he would turn, to the left or the right. He lengthened his own strides. He wasn't going to turn. There was a bench just before the railing. He leapt to the bench, from there onto the railing, and then out into the open air.

He reached the opposite railing easily, landing one foot on it briefly before he tumbled over. There was no bench on that side and he fell heavily to the stone floor, scrambling up again immediately to check to his left and right.

If his cousins had guessed what he intended, they might have sent someone ahead to spoil his moment of triumph, but there was no sign of pursuit. He could turn back to savor his victory.

The light well was narrow but long. By the time his cousins had run around it—whichever way they chose to go—Gen would be safely away. They all knew it, and had panted to a halt in front of the bench. None of them dared attempt the jump. They sent threats across the open space instead.

There were so many things Gen wanted to shout back that he couldn't settle on any one of them, so he put his thumbs in his ears and stuck out his tongue. When a heavy hand fell on his shoulder and he whirled around in panic.

"Sten," he gasped. "Gods, you scared me."

His older brother, Stenides, stood behind him. His expression was stern, but Gen was delighted and turned back to his pursuers more cocksure than before. He put his thumbs back in his ears. He couldn't open the fingers on his right hand to achieve an entirely satisfying wave, and he had no sooner begun to waggle the fingers of the other hand when Stenides shook him hard. Both his hands dropped.

"What's he done?"

Gen turned on his brother, speechless with outrage, while Cleon, the leader among his cousins, answered from across the light well.

"Sten, he's taken Breia's earrings. The gold ones Father gave her for her birthday."

They were beautiful earrings, gold set with crystal and onyx. Too valuable, really, for a girl of thirteen. To have taken them was far more than a child's prank. Stenides looked down at his brother unhappily.

"Ask him why," Gen said, as angry as he had been exuberant only a moment before.

Stenides turned to Cleon, and Cleon threw up his hands. "Because he's a little savage and someone should have wrung his neck years ago, why else?" Cleon shouted. The cousins loudly supported him.

Gen shouted back, his shrill voice cutting across their deeper ones. "Because she said that if Father hadn't married so far beneath himself, he could have made himself king!"

Gen felt Stenides stiffen beside him, and the boys on the far side of the light well were abruptly silent. Certain only a moment before that they were securely in the right, they suddenly suspected they might be deeply in the wrong. Even Cleon. If his sister Breia had, in fact, insulted their cousins' family, then it was Stenides who was going to come around the light well with grim purpose in mind.

Timos, Tenris, and the others shuffled their feet nervously. Together, they could beat Stenides . . . if they chose to. But that would mean supporting Breia's insult, and only a fool would do that. Breia was a mealy-mouthed little shrew, and she'd overstepped herself. The king of Eddis was ill and both his sons dead. He had only daughters to inherit unless one of his brothers seized the throne. With her sniping comment, Breia had insulted not only Gen's mother, who was the daughter of the king's Thief and, strictly speaking, not a member of a landholding family, but also Gen's father, implying that he would consider denying his niece her rightful inheritance. This kind of insult dragged whole families into feuds that lasted for years.

Cleon looked appalled. Then he shrugged an apology. "I'm sorry, Sten," he said. "I had no idea. I'll talk to Father and he'll talk to Breia."

The cousins bobbed their heads and melted away.

Stenides turned to his little brother.

"You're lucky, whelp," he said. "If I hadn't been here, they would have pounded you to mush and taken the earrings back." Gen's theft would have been politely overlooked once the earrings were safely returned, and no one would have heard any more of Breia's insulting words.

"If they'd caught me," said Gen.

"Which they would have."

"Would not," Gen protested. "I would have disappeared like that"—he snapped his fingers—"before they were halfway around the light well."

"You would have hopped it?"

"Yes!"

"That's why you've been standing on one foot this whole time."

Gen stuck out his chin and put his sore foot on the ground, but he didn't put any weight on it. He'd twisted his ankle falling from the wall. As the excitement faded, it was beginning to hurt quite a bit.

Stenides smiled at him and then turned to offer him a ride on his back.

"You're an idiot," Sten said.

"Breia should have her lips sewed shut," said Gen.

"She'll probably wish she had before her father's through with her." Breia's insults would be officially forgotten . . . but nonetheless discussed in scandalized whispers by everyone in the palace. So long as Gen left the jewelry on an altar, dedicated to a god or goddess, where it could never be retrieved by the original owner or by himself, no criticism would come his way.

He was holding the earrings so tightly in his right hand that he could feel their sides digging into his palm, and he suspected their delicate wires would be badly bent before he got them to the temple.

"He's not going to give her another set of earrings, that's for certain," said Gen with great satisfaction.

Stenides sighed. "If you had just told me . . ."

"If I had told you, you would have told Cleon, and he would have made her apologize, and she would have smiled with all her teeth showing and said, 'Oh, I am so sorry, of course I was just joking. . . .' And she was not joking *at all*," said Gen.

Stenides came to a staircase. "Do you want to go dedicate them now?" he asked.

Gen had to think for a minute before he answered. The boys' dormitory would be empty in the middle of the afternoon. He needn't dedicate the earrings immediately.

"Do you want to go lie down for a while?" Stenides asked, sensing his hesitation.

"Yes, please," said Gen.

"All right then." Stenides started up the stairs. He took Gen all the way to his cot and laid him gently on it. He ruffled his younger brother's hair. "Cleon would have been very sorry after he'd pounded you to mush, but Lader wouldn't have been," he said. "You want to watch out for him."

Gen looked up at his brother. Stenides was one of his favorite people, certainly his favorite sibling. Like Gen, Stenides didn't fit well into his martial world. He had a gift for the mechanical and the mathematical. It was Stenides who had taught his younger brother to read and was most often to be found absorbed in his unwarlike hobby of watch-making. Yet in spite of being different, Stenides was well-liked. Gen sighed.

"Did you see my jump?" he asked hopefully.

"Gods, yes, I did," said Stenides. "I thought I'd never exhale again. What possessed you to do something that stupid?"

"It wasn't stupid."

"You might have been killed."

"How?" Gen asked, genuinely surprised.

Stenides looked at him in horror. "Do you mean to say that you've done that before?"

"Of course."

Stenides was struck dumb, but only momentarily. "Gen, did Grandfather teach you to do that?"

Gen looked away. "I'm going to be the Thief of Eddis," he said.

Sitting on the bed beside him, Stenides said very carefully, "Gen. You shouldn't listen to the stories he tells you. Being the Thief . . . It's just a leftover title from ancient history. It doesn't mean anything anymore."

Gen only looked stubborn, and Stenides was wise enough to give up an argument he knew he couldn't win. "Well," Sten said. "Promise me at least that you won't go jumping across any more light wells."

Gen didn't want to fight with his brother. "All right," he agreed easily.

"Good enough," said Stenides, and then he went away.

Gen lay back on his cot and examined the earrings he'd snatched from Breia's jewel case, turning them this way and that, straightening the wires where they had bent. His grandfather usually stole cloak pins to leave on the altar of the God of Thieves. Admiring the way the light sparkled in the bits of crystal, Gen decided he preferred to steal earrings.

He'd lied to Stenides. Of course he was going to continue jumping across light wells. Someday, he promised himself, he *would* be the next Thief of Eddis.

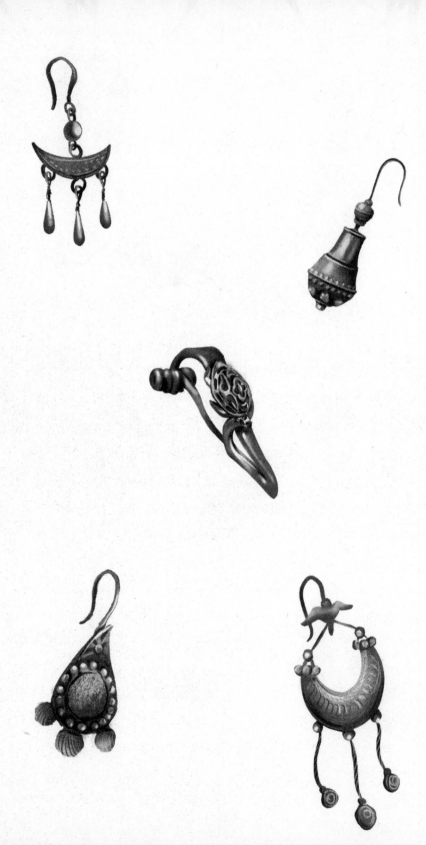

⯈· FIBULA PINS ·⯇

While Gen was fascinated from an early age by earrings, his grandfather had a predilection for large fibula pins used to fasten cloaks. The first ones I saw were in the collection of the Metropolitan Museum of Art in New York City. I've always wondered if they are called fibula pins because they are so similar to the bones in our lower legs, or if that's what we call the bones in our lower legs because they look so much like the pins.

The first fibula pins were crafted at the end of the Neolithic period—they were an improvement over straight pins for holding your clothes together. While we use buttons more often, safety pins in the same shape are still around.

Irene's education will bear bitter fruit. There is sweetness there, even so.

Burning Down the House of Kallicertes

Irene was listening with only half an ear to Relius. Her face to the window, bathed in the sun, she was thinking of all the men already dead, as well as those taken prisoner. Tall and short, generous and mean, cowardly or brave. Some had fought from duty and some with a vengeance. Did any of them, she wondered, carve small wooden figurines? Were they poets, did they whistle in tune? How many of them were fathers and how many had daughters they loved and who loved them in return? Relius was telling her that all of them, the musical and the tone-deaf alike, must die or be sold as slaves. He'd in fact stopped talking and was patiently waiting for her agreement. A bastard by lineage and a cynic by nature, he did not put much value on life.

Irene turned away from the window. "Send a third of the prisoners to the mines," she said. "Sell a third to the slavers and exile the rest. Any who have the means may buy their freedom. We can use the coin."

Gently, or gently for him, Relius said, "My queen, your mercy is admirable—" before breaking off.

What incredible power was in the tap of a fingernail against the polished wooden arm of her chair, Irene thought. Men, even her teachers, spoke with her leave, were silent at her command.

"We will break up the estate," said Irene. "And give a piece to each, Susa, Laimonides, and Erondites."

"But Erondites expects the whole, Your Majesty," Relius warned.

"Does he?"

"You promised to uphold his legal claim on it."

"Did I?"

Relius considered and, after consideration, conceded. Irene had made no promises, only kept her own counsel as the Baron's assumptions had run away with him. "*Erondites* believes you have promised to uphold his claim."

"*Erondites* is mistaken," said the queen, showing her teeth.

Relius offered his own sly smile in return. She might silence him with a gesture, but she was still his student and he a proud mentor. "He will continue to assert in the courts that it belongs to his family by right of prior claim," mused Relius. "There will be legal challenges for years."

"Hmm," said the queen lightly, turning back to the window. "Give that pretty little villa on the Pelean tributary to Susa," she said over her shoulder.

"And the main house?"

"Burn it."

Even Relius was shocked. The villa was old—ancient—and unrivaled in its beauty, filled with art, marbled columns and mosaic floors. Hundreds of years of careful management had gone into the expansive gardens surrounding it.

"Tear the buildings to the ground," said Irene. "Cut down every tree, grub up every living thing. There is to be no stone unturned. And when you're done, pile the wood into whatever remains of the house, and then I want it to burn. I want it to burn for *days*."

Relius looked stricken. She almost laughed. Somewhere inside him still was the son of a steward whose sacred trust was the preservation of *property*, who would see a thousand men dead, but go all weak and trembling at the idea of destroying a great work of art.

The smoke from that house's funeral pyre would be seen for miles. The whole world would know of its utter, unrelenting destruction. Let Erondites and Susa squabble in court over the remains, the longer the better. Or maybe Laimonides would claw the land out from under both of them, she didn't care. None of it would never go back to its former owners. Their famous home and all their wealth would be gone, nothing left of the villa of so many stories, nothing left of its divine mosaics, its cool elegant rooms, its lofty halls, its expansive baths. That place where she had been so miserable, so weak, so despised, would be nothing but ashes and rubble, an otherwise empty field scattered in the springtime with bloodred poppies.

They would hate her for destroying it, all those men who would otherwise have died, all those women who would have lost husbands and sons and brothers. All those dutiful daughters who might have seen their father's headless corpses in the dirt. They would hate her forever—let them hate her for something she would never regret. The house of Kallicertes would not rise again.

"Relius," she said, calling her adviser back from the doorway. She'd been staring out the window so long, he'd quietly excused himself. "There's a bank of coleus along the east side of the garden."

"Yes, my queen?"

"Leave it untouched."

⊱· BEE PENDANT ·⊰

This is the model for the royal bee earrings that Irene used to finance her rise to power. It's a pendant that was found in Malia on Crete and is displayed in the museum in Heraklion. No one can be sure if these are really bees or mammoth wasps, if that's pollen dropping from their wings or something else entirely. It was made sometime in the seventeenth or eighteenth or nineteenth century BCE, and I saw it the first time in 1992—so, more than three thousand years after a jeweler fused each of those tiny gold beads in place in a process called granulation.

Gen is clever, but not yet wise. He has much to lose before he gains wisdom.

The Watch Takes the Thief

Hearing the watchman hesitantly shuffling his sandals in the doorway, Tertix didn't look up. "What is it now?" he snapped, his attention on the paper in front of him, covered with inkblots and scratched-out words. As the watch leader, his was the job of recording any arrests, and he was making slow work of it. He would have to recopy the whole thing once he decided what to write.

"It's that thief, sir."

That brought Tertix's head up. "If he has escaped—"

"No, no, sir, nothing like that."

Tertix dropped his face into his palms. They'd spent what had felt like hours chasing the little demon all over the city as he fled across the rooftops and slid down drainpipes only to turn up again in plain sight. He'd thrown garbage at them, emptied slop pots—the whole sorry business was written out on the paper on Tertix's desk. There

was no point in obfuscation. There were too many witnesses. Every wineshop in the city had been emptied, their
clientele out in the streets cheering the little monster on.

"If he has not escaped, why are you here?" Maybe they
murdered him, Tertix thought.

"We searched him again, and—"

"No." He'd already finished inventorying everything
they'd piled on his desk earlier—overwhelming evidence of
an expansive crime spree, and yet another indict-
ment of the watch. "Why did you do that?"

"The . . . the prisoner had been acting . . .
suspiciously."

The prisoner had been acting suspiciously if by suspiciously
one meant laughing and making airy references to incompe-
tent clods. He'd gone on laughing right up until Proliteus
had punched him in the chest. After that, he'd rolled around
on the floor gasping for breath while they pulled off all
his clothes and went over every inch of their seams,
pinching and twisting to check for items still hidden in tiny pockets in the cloth. And then when
they were *sure* they'd found everything, Proliteus
had realized what the thief was saying between
gasps: "B-b-buttons."

"We found these," he

said, adding a handful of items to the pile already on the desk. "Then we . . . uh . . ."

Murdered him.

"Thought maybe we should check the buttons on his tunic."

Three of the buttons had turned out to be silver when they scraped the blacking off. Proliteus had almost kicked the little thief again. They'd given him back his pants and his hideous yellow shirt, but they'd torn the tunic to pieces.

Proliteus had been stuck with the job of taking their findings to the watch leader, one of the younger sons of the city's patronoi, who took the job in turns.

"My gods," whispered Tertix, "is that a *toothbrush*?"

The watchman winced. "I think it's the king's," he said.

"It can't be."

"It's—it's got a little lion on it." Proliteus pointed.

Indeed, when Tertix held it up to his nose, he could see on the black lacquer handle a tiny gold-leaf lion of Sounis, crouched to spring.

The watchman next pointed his blunt fingertip at a delicate wire earring. "I think that belongs to Lady Melinna, and that one is . . . I think it's the one the minister of the navy said was stolen last week. He accused one of his servants of taking it."

Next to the earring was a fibula with a distinctive

worked-turtle decoration. The turtle was a sym-
bol of strength and a token in Tertix's family. "That's . . . that's my father's pin!"
He looked up at the watchman in
horror. "That thief has been all
over the megaron. He's been everywhere."

The watchman nodded uncomfortably. "So, so, so."

"When people find out . . ." Tertix's thoughts turned
again to murder. "Is he *trying* to get himself killed?"

"Some of these people, sir, they just want to be famous."

"Well, he's certainly going to be *that*."

>· THE LION GATE ·<

When I first saw the Lion Gate, in 1993, guidebooks said
it had been discovered by the nineteenth-century archeologist Heinrich Schliemann. That's not really accurate. Unlike
many artifacts which disappeared over the years, the Lion
Gate was never fully buried. Schliemann didn't need to
dig it up and lots of people knew already what it was. In
fact, Pausanias, a Greek writer in the second century CE,
described it so well that in 1700 an engineer working on a

register of the properties in the Peloponnese was easily able to identify it as the citadel of Mycenae.

Over time, though, the significance of the gate and the citadel had been lost; it was the interest in these ruins that Heinrich Schliemann kindled. Fascinated since childhood by *The Iliad* and *The Odyssey*, Schliemann believed that Homer's story of Helen of Troy was based on historical events, that there was once a city on the shores of what is now Turkey that was besieged by armies from the Peloponnese in Greece. A wealthy man, Schliemann could fund his own archeological excavations. After discovering what he claimed was the site of the historical Troy, he went on to search for Mycenae, the city of Agamemnon, the high king and leader of the city-states of the Peloponnese and there, as plain as the nose on your face, was the Lion Gate.

The gate dates to the fourteenth century BCE. The figures on either side of the pillar may be lions, or not. Their heads were made separately, and they are missing. Some think the figures were sphinxes with their heads turned to watch the people approaching the city.

Mortal minds perceive the gods as reflections on water. Without the Gift, the water moves; the image is lost. All things made are unmade.

The Destruction of Hamiathes's Gift

Around the porches of the main temple of Hephestia torches blazed, obscuring the light of the stars overhead. More torches lined the path of the Sacred Way as it led down into the city of Eddis, across the valley and up the distant slopes of the sacred mountain. The Queen's Thief of Eddis stood in the doorway of the temple and wondered how many torches there were. The temple workers had been driving the stakes for their supports for days. The priests had left at sunset, lighting each torch as they passed it. The Thief had not envied them their journey, balancing dignity against haste as they strove to reach the end of their path before too much of the night was gone.

As the light had faded from the sky, it had been possible to track their progress. The twin rows of torches melted into a single glowing track on the far side of the city, and that line grew fainter and fainter in the distance until no mortal eye could have distinguished the moment the light bearers reached their destination at the lip of the Hephestial crater were it not for the greater light of the signal beacon that began to burn. It would soon be time for the royal procession to begin.

The Queen of Eddis, accompanied by a large crowd of her own people, as well as the representatives from countries near and far, would follow the path of the torches and, surrounded by witnesses, throw Hamiathes's Gift into the fires of the Sacred Mountain to be destroyed. Unlike the poor priests and priestesses rushing along on foot, the Queen and her escort would ride until they reached the slopes of the Sacred Mountain.

The Queen's Thief stopped jingling the odds and ends in his pockets and turned back into the temple to join the people milling inside. He was to ride beside and just behind his Queen. She had met all his protests with her gentlest and least alterable insistence and she knew he would not disappoint her.

The night was clear and the mountain air chilly. The torches on either side of the procession left everyone night blind, making it a frustrating and very boring ride to the bare slopes of Hephestia's mountain. Behind the Queen of Eddis and her Thief came her ministers and visiting dignitaries, including the Queen of Attolia and the King of Sounis, Eddis's immediate neighbors. Sounis had brought his heir. The more powerful countries of the continent had sent ambassadors to represent the heads of state who could not condescend to attend in person the backward religious festival of a tiny country like Eddis.

As the procession climbed onto the rocky fields above the tree line, the sky lightened. The procession reached the lip of the crater as the first slanting rays of the sun lit the steam rising from the Hephestial fire deep in the crater at the top of the mountain.

Eddis dressed in the Continental style—her dress of beautiful fabric, but very plain. Her Thief was more traditionally dressed, like most of the Eddisian men, in an embroidered velvet overshirt, pants that belled at the ankles before being tucked into low boots. From farther back in the procession, the Queen of Attolia was watching him closely. The velvet of his overshirt was midnight blue, so dark as to appear black before the sun rose. The embroidery was silver and gold and bright blue silk. His dark hair was pulled back from his face and braided. The scar on his face was healed and white against his light brown skin.

At the lip of the crater, the procession spread out. Before them the ground dropped steeply and disappeared several hundred yards below into the mist. The far side of the crater was hazy. Most of the people were watching Eddis, but the Queen of Attolia, Eddis noted, continued to watch the Thief.

Eddis removed the stone that was Hamiathes's Gift from

where it hung on a short gold wire from the torque around her neck. A priestess stepped over to the Queen and handed her an elaborately carved but obviously functional crossbow. Eddis said something under her breath to her Thief and he ducked his head momentarily. When he lifted it again, his engaging smile was just fading. Throwing Hamiathes's Gift into the Hephestial Fire had seemed a straightforward and simple proposition when the Queen had first mentioned it. Like most such dramatic actions it turned out to be more complicated. No one had seen the Hephestial Fire at the bottom of the crater, or at least no one who had lived to tell about it. The inner slope of the crater was steep, but not vertical. In the event that the stone, thrown into the mist, landed instead on the slope below and hung up on an outcropping, what then? A foolhardy individual who climbed down the inner edge of the crater would almost certainly be overcome by the fumes, but any who lived to climb out again, carrying Hamiathes's Gift, would also carry the Goddess-given right to choose the next ruler of Eddis. It would be a powerful and enduring temptation.

Even at the lip, the air was difficult to breathe, the fumes rasping in the throats of the onlookers, and drifting billows of gray steam made all but the priests and priestesses cough. Nonetheless, the possibility of the successful fool could not be discounted, nor the possibility for fraud. In appearance the Gift was unremarkable. It could be almost any small stone picked from a riverbed with a hole bored through it and a few shallow runes carved in its side.

Indeed, the Queen of Eddis had enjoyed watching the faces of the representatives of foreign courts as they had approached her throne where she sat with the Gift hanging from the gold torque, watching their disdain at its dull aspect turn to shock and then to wonder. It was Hamiathes's Gift, given to him by the Great Goddess, and in its presence there was no room for any doubt of its authenticity.

Sadly, away from the Gift, the wonder soon faded, leaving only the memory of a rather ordinary water-smoothed stone incongruously dangling from a golden wire and an ornately worked torque. Eddis's Thief believed that all sense of the Gift's power would be forgotten the moment it was destroyed, making a fraud easy to perpetrate. There could be no uncertainty left in the eyes of the witnesses to tempt treasure seekers and undermine Eddis's rule. Nor, as importantly, did Eddis wish to see numerous people go to their deaths trying to retrieve it when all she wanted was to see the thing destroyed.

"Use a slingshot," her Thief had suggested, and the Queen had laughed at the image of herself, in her most awe-inspiring finery in front of the delegates and rulers from the surrounding countries, swinging a strap over her head and letting the stone fly from its pocket. The crossbow was a slightly more dignified alternative, but it still struck the Queen as vaguely ridiculous and she had said as much to her Thief.

Resting the already cocked weapon in the crook of one arm she held out her hand to receive the crossbow bolt. In concert the visiting dignitaries looked from her hand to the crater and back to her hand. This would be an awkward time to fumble the small stone, but Eddis had practiced for hours in the safety of the courtyard. Using a dummy, an ordinary stone the same size and weight as the Gift, she had fired the crossbow with the stone attached in several different ways until she and her engineers had been certain the weight would not drop off in an accidental and disastrous way.

Eddis slid the wire that ran through the center of the Gift through a ring at the head of the bolt and twisted the soft gold tight, then she slid the bolt into the groove waiting to receive it. She raised the crossbow to her shoulder, pointed it high into the air, and fired.

The king of Sounis watched with bitter hunger as the shot, carrying its burden, leapt into the air. *His* magus had located the stone, had held the stone in his hand, and then had lost it. The stone, by rights, should have been Sounis's. The rule of Eddis and the immortality it promised should have been his. Had they been, no one would have seen him throwing away the gift of the Great Goddess. It mattered little to Sounis, in fact he hardly noticed, that the great goddess was not worshipped in his country, that until he had seen the gift for himself he hadn't believed in her, or for that matter in any god. Having seen the gift he believed in it wholeheartedly and seeing it begin to drop into the center of the crater made him want to bellow his frustration.

Along with the King of Sounis, the priests and priestesses and onlookers, the representatives of foreign heads of state and the powerful Trading Houses, all watched the bolt dropping lower and lower into the mist.

Only Attolia had not taken her eyes off the Thief, so she saw the Queen of Eddis sag as the shot left the crossbow, and saw the Thief catch at the fabric at the back of her dress until Eddis straightened and stood again. Attolia supposed that giving up one's guarantee of immortality would be a blow. She wondered what foolish notions had motivated the Queen of Eddis to do so.

Turning her eyes she scanned the mist until she saw the bolt fading from sight in the depths of the crater. All eyes except the Thief's were on it. Even when it was invisible to the keenest eye, they stood searching for it in the wisps of steam, each wondering how they would know when the stone reached the fire. The Thief knew. He alone turned away from the crater and looked instead from face to face, pausing at last on the Queen of Attolia. He knew the moment Hamiathes's Gift reached the Hephestial Fire, knew the moment it ceased to exist. He saw its destruction reflected in the face of the Queen as her fierce belief in the Gift faded away.

⟩· THE MOLOSSIAN HOUND ·⟨

I am pretty sure this sculpture was labeled The Molossian Hound when I first saw it in the British Museum, but it's also known as the Jennings Dog, the Duncombe Dog, and the Dog of Alcibiades. The first two are people who owned the statue. The third, Alcibiades, lived in Athens in the fifth century BCE. There's a story about him buying a dog with a particularly fine tail and then having the tail docked. When his friends told him that was ridiculous, he said he hoped to give people in Athens something to talk about besides him. When Henry Constantine Jennings bought the sculpture in Rome in the eighteenth century, he noticed it was missing its tail and remembered the story. Jennings thought the statue was from the same era as the famous Athenian, so he called it Alcibiades's Dog, but it is a Roman copy of a Hellenistic bronze, which means Jennings was off by several hundred years at least.

The British Museum describes it as a guard dog, but Molossians were evidently used for hunting. What better dog, I thought, to hunt a Thief?

⤷· IN THE QUEEN'S PRISON ·⤶

Oxe Harbrea

Onus Savonus

God of thieves

Offend the gods–

Love is what

She and I

Dancer in

Moving, lovely,

Earrings for

Sacrus Vax Dragga

Sophos at Ere

my betrayer

now I see

I sent my queen

in the garden

the palace garden

can you love me?

your mortal beauty

Earrings for	your nighttime table
Earrings for	my stealthy dream
Gods of Eddis—	now I fathom
Thief of Eddis—	now I see
Mother, Father—	you should have told me
Love is what	offends the gods
Oxe Harbrea	Sacrus Vax Dragga
Onus Savonus	Sophos at Ere

Relius and Teleus move pieces in a game,
knowing they themselves are pieces in a game.

The Games of Kings

Relius toppled his king. "Your game," he said to Teleus, looking over the wasteland of the board. His thoughts had been elsewhere, and he was down to only a pawn and a rook. He tipped his head back to drain the last of the wine from his cup as he stood.

"Stay," said Teleus, on impulse.

Relius smirked. "I have a wife waiting for me, remember?"

Teleus shook his head.

"What?" said Relius. "You have your women in the town."

"Not married ones."

"And that delightful boy in the fifth who makes such eyes at you," Relius added, mimicking the doelike expression of a besotted teen.

"I do not rob cradles," snapped the captain of the guard.

"Whyever not?" Relius shot back.

"Maybe because I don't enjoy being hunted down by their angry mothers—or *aunts*," said Teleus.

"That only happened once."

Teleus raised an eyebrow, and Relius laughed. "All right, once was more than enough. But you should be more careful yourself, my friend. Our new king is so very young—remarks about cradle robbing might not be well received."

Teleus didn't laugh. "He is only waiting for an opportunity," he warned.

Relius shrugged, a wordless concession.

"Don't give him one, you idiot."

The toppled pieces on the chessboard were suddenly intriguing to Relius. He lifted piece after piece, restoring each to its place. He didn't want to talk about inevitabilities, not with Teleus, so he said, "That's why I don't understand all your fearmongering about other men's wives. Better one of my lovers gets me killed before the king of Attolia does. Don't you think?"

"You're assuming it has to be one or the other."

"You mean it could be both? That's a horrible thought, Teleus. You know, you only think like that when you're tired. For gods' sakes, get some rest." Relius lifted his cup again, remembered it was empty, and set it back on the table. Then he laid his hand on the captain's shoulder. "Good night, my friend," he said, more seriously. "I'll do my best to be circumspect."

Teleus sat alone at the chessboard long after he was gone, idly arranging and rearranging the pieces, as if looking for a solution to an invisible checkmate.

*"Sometimes, if you want to change
a man's mind, you have to change
the mind of the man next to him first."*

⤜· VAPHEIO CUPS ·⤛

When I wrote the scene where Costis promises ten gold cups for the altar in *The King of Attolia*, and then briefly considers substituting much smaller ceremonial cups instead, these are the cups I had in mind. I saw them displayed in the National Archeological Museum in Athens. They come from the Vapheio excavations not very far from Mycenae, from a tomb excavated in 1889 by Christos Tsountas.

The pottery in the tomb dates to the middle of the second millennium BCE, but these gold cups might be older. Some scholars think one was made on the mainland and the other was Minoan, made on the island of Crete. The cups are so famous that all cups of this shape, including pottery ones, are called Vapheio cups.

Druic will dance for the king and learn how dangerous it is to disappoint Eugenides.

Knife Dance

"My brother can do the Eddisian knife dance!"

The official from the palace looked skeptical. Tasked with finding entertainers to perform at the upcoming feast of Cerulis, he'd been scouting among the troupes of players, jugglers, dancers, and acrobats who had camped on the open marshy ground near the Tustis River. They had come, as they did every year, to exchange news and recruit new company members and to make money at the festival. For three days, wealthy citizens and guilds would fund performances at their homes or their meetinghouses or their Ceruliums—where the more exclusive societies met to worship. The best performers would be invited to demonstrate their skill before the king and queen, and the very best of those would be awarded the Cerulis medal at the end of the feast. The official, surrounded by a crowd of people eager to have a chance at the prize, was doling out tokens for an opportunity to audition.

He had a limited number and didn't recognize the man in

76

front of him. He wasn't from any of the well-known troupes. Stocky, middle-aged, with slightly battered features, he wasn't any sort of a dancer or acrobat himself. His brother standing just behind him, was slighter of build, and could have been a dancer. He was plucking at the larger man's sleeve.

"Ruk, are you sure . . . ?"

But Ruk brushed him off. "The king's Eddisian, so?" he said. "He'll like an Eddisian dance."

The official, about to turn away, hesitated. It was true that the king was Eddisian and might be particularly pleased by a traditional dance from his home.

"There's not another man in Attolia, maybe not even in Eddis, who can do the knife dance, so. It's one of the Mysteries of the Thieves, so. Five knives. All at once. My brother knows the whole thing."

"Is that true?" the representative asked the timid man.

"So, so," he said, "but . . ."

It was worth a token. The others all had gone to people from troupes that had won the Cerulis medal in the past; if the anxious little man couldn't live up to his brother's big-mouth promises, there were plenty of other seasoned performers to choose from. The representative handed Ruk the token and moved on.

"Ruk, are you mad?" said Druic. "Why not just tell him I can see the future while you were at it?"

"Because you can't see the future."

"I can't do the knife dance, either. Father never taught me."

"You watched him every day for your entire life and I've seen you hiding behind the wagon practicing. You'll be fine."

"What if I don't know all the steps? What if I've got it wrong?"

Ruk threw up his hands. "For crying out loud, Druic. We agreed to come to the Cerulis to try to get a place with one of the big troupes. How the hell did you think we were going to do that if you don't do the knife dance? Did you think anyone needs another juggler spinning plates on a stick?"

Druic hunched his shoulders. "Father said never to do the knife dance."

"Father's dead. To hell with father. I am sick of trekking through the backwoods trying to make it on our own."

Druic shook his head helplessly. His brother got drunk and got in fights and that was why they traveled on their own. That's why they were so often chased out of town after a single performance. Druic's juggling skills could have gotten them a place at any mid-sized troupe, but he didn't have a skill amazing enough to overcome Ruk's reputation.

"I don't have any knives," Druic said.

"Use Father's."

"I buried them."

"Buried them where?"

"With him, where do you think?"

"Why would you do that? No, never mind, don't tell me. You're an idiot, that's why. Who cares? We'll get you a set of wooden ones."

"Wood?"

"We'll paint them. No one will know."

The audition went perfectly. Ruk, when he was sober, had the attention to detail of a successful con man. The knives he painted looked impressively sharp from a distance, and Druic loved to perform. All of his shyness and timidity fell away once he was out in front of a crowd. He only wished he could hold on to that confidence once his performance was over. The days of waiting after the audition and before the Cerulis feast were a living hell. He picked at his fingers, picked at his food, sat hunched over the terrible queasiness in his stomach, while Ruk tried to encourage him with a steady stream of abuse. "For Gods' sakes, sit up and stop whimpering. I will smack you, you know. I don't know why I saddle myself with you, so you just remember this is your last chance."

The banquet hall was filled. All the members of the court who could fit were crowded together on the benches that lined the walls. The king and queen sat in gold thrones on a raised stage with their attendants seated on the steps leading up to it. Druic stood alone, in the open space before them. He took a deep breath and displayed his five wooden knives in a precise fan, then snapped the fan closed again. He slid one blade across the tiny bladder of red paint he had hidden in his hand and showed the bright red "blood" to the audience. Then he threw all the knives into the air.

The knives went up as if on wings, each to a different height, and as they dropped he twisted and caught them, flipping them up again and again, all the while stepping in an intricate pattern around a center point in a repeating loop like a figure eight. Every throw was perfect, every catch was flawless right up until he turned and found himself face to face with the king of Attolia.

The knives fell to the ground, clattering like the fakes they were against the marble floor. The king looked at them, craning his head to see each one. All of Druic's fears flooded back.

The king toed the knife by his foot.

"Did your father teach you this dance?" he asked calmly.

"N-no, Your Majesty. The man who taught it to him made him promise never to teach it to anyone else."

"Then how do you know it?"

"I watched my father and copied it on my own."

"Ah. That explains the mistakes." He looked at the knives. "They're wood."

Druic nodded. There was no point in denying it.

"I thought maybe you didn't have a set of real ones," said the king. "I was going to offer to let you use mine."

In the crook of his elbow was a narrow wooden box. Breathless, Druic watched the king as he lifted off the top to show five beautiful and no doubt razor-sharp knives nestled like a school of lean and silvery fish on the blue velvet inside.

"I sent someone to fetch them when I heard you would perform the knife dance."

The king offered him the box. Druic shook his head, backed away. He tried to bluff. "It has to be done with wood knives, Your Majesty." Many of the moves didn't involve catching the knife by the handle, or even by the blade. Instead the flat of the blade had to be bounced off the back of the knuckles. Even a slight mistake might cost a finger or all the tendons in one hand. That was why Druic had buried his father with his knives. He thought he would never have the skill to use them.

"Oh," said the king in dire tones. "Let me show you how it's done." He handed Druic the knife case and positioned him just so. "Hold very still," he whispered in Druic's ear and plucked the knives out of the velvet. He tucked four under his arm and tossed the remaining one into the air, holding his hand flat underneath it as it fell. The knife blade hit his hand just a moment before his fingers closed on it and a thin red line sprang up, his sacrifice to his god.

Then he danced.

Afraid to lose an ear, or worse, Druic couldn't even turn his head to watch as the knives rose and fell around him. At first there was an occasional ring of metal on metal as the knives hit against the hook the king wore in place of a hand, but that sound faded and all Druic could hear was his own heartbeat banging away in his ears as the king spun front and back, pulling the knives out of the air and throwing them up again until Druic, subsisting on only the shallowest of breaths, thought he might die if the dance didn't end soon. Finally, Eugenides halted in front of him. With a last flick of his wrist, he sent the knives up and not one came down.

Swallowing the lump in his throat, Druic lifted his eyes to see the impossible. All five knives stuck in the ceiling high overhead. Eugenides put his hands on either side of Druic's face and pulled him close to whisper in his ear, "Never dance for *me* again with wooden knives."

The movement of Druic's head wasn't so much a shake as a quiver. "I won't. I swear I won't," he said.

The king stepped back. The knives dropped down. In one motion, he swept them from the air and smiled at Druic as he replaced them in their box, then watched approvingly as Druic put the lid back on.

"Come sit with me," said the king, and without waiting to see if Druic followed, he walked back to his throne.

Two of the attendants made room and Druic sat on the step of the dais, near the king's feet, for the rest of the performances. He watched the archway through which the artists came and went for some sign of his brother, but he didn't doubt that Ruk had fled the palace the moment the knives had hit the ground, if not the moment the king had left his throne. Ruk would have seen him moving, though Druic had not.

In between the performances, the king chatted, asked about Kathodicia, where Druic was from. Asked about Druic's father, who had died the winter before of a fever. Asked about Ruk and his plan to join one of the troupes at the Cerulis festival.

"He doesn't perform himself?"

"No, Your Majesty. He's a laborer."

"But he makes the plans?"

"He always has. My father favored him."

"I see," said the king. "Maybe of the two of you, Ruk needed it more. Did your father tell you, when he was dying, that you should stay with your brother?"

"No," said Druic, staring glumly at the pattern in the marble under his feet. "He told me not to do the knife dance."

The king laughed. "You should have listened more carefully. My god does not tolerate missteps."

Druic didn't remember a single performance that followed. The evening was a blur of light and sound and what he mostly remembered later were the patterns in the marble tiles on the floor. Blocks of geometric patterns to represent waves, others with fish or dolphins, one with an octopus, its eight tentacles curling in all directions. He did listen to the king and queen talking, though, when the performers were done and the judges were choosing a winner.

"You seem to know Kathodicia well," said the queen to the king.

"I visited with my grandfather when I was very small. We stayed longer than expected," he told her.

She raised an eyebrow.

"I fell off a horse—broke both my arms." The king sounded embarrassed.

"You fell?" The queen sounded gently amazed. If she was amazed, Druic was stunned. He lifted his head and looked at the king, who nodded down at him.

"My grandfather was *livid*. I ruined all of his plans and we had to find someone to take us in, as he had no way to pay for our keep while I healed."

Just then, the judges returned to announce the winner of the medal, and the king finally excused Druic, sending him to get a dinner he hadn't earned and couldn't eat, along with the other performers, while the winner of the Cerulis medal, a piper, approached the throne to receive his prize.

"No," said Druic, the next afternoon. His brother wanted him to add the knife dance as a regular part of his routine, and he refused. He'd never refused Ruk anything, not really. He'd always given in, but he knew this time he wouldn't. "The king didn't even let me finish."

"He was going to let you use his knives! If you weren't such a cursed coward you'd have the Cerulis medal right now. Do the knife dance and you can pick any troupe you want."

"I can't do it with real knives. I don't know all the throws."

"We'll make another set of wooden ones."

"No. I told you. Eugenides told me not to dance for him with wooden knives."

"The king's never going to know!"

"*You don't understand,*" shouted Druic, tongue-tied. Unable to put what he'd felt into words.

"No, I don't understand!" Ruk poked Druic hard in the chest. "The only thing you do that's worth doing is that knife dance and if you won't do it, I am done with you. Done. You'll be on your own. You just think about that while I go get a drink." He stormed away, slamming the door behind him.

Druic knew that one drink would turn into many, would turn into a bar fight, would turn into a night in the city's gaol. He sat down on the narrow cot in the tiny room they shared at the Cerulis Inn, picked for its lucky name. They'd sold their wagon and the horse to come to the capital. He'd loved the horse and now they had nothing but the clothes that lay scattered on the floor, and the bag of juggling props. Ruk had all their money, and it would soon be gone. Druic had always given way to Ruk, always let Ruk do the talking, always let Ruk make the plans. The truth was that Druic relied on Ruk to handle all the things that frightened him. But he remembered how Eugenides's hands had felt on either side of his face. Two hands, when the king had only one. Druic knew he'd never risk the knife dance again.

Ruk returned to the inn late the next day, nursing bruises and a headache. He found the room empty, only his own clothes on the floor. When he stumped back down the stairs to ask the innkeeper where his idiot brother might be, the man handed him a small bag of coins.

"An advance on your brother's pay," said the innkeeper. "He left it here for you."

"What pay?"

"He joined a troupe of players. They left the city this morning."

"Which one?" asked Ruk, thinking he would have to move fast to catch up.

"He didn't say."

*"If I am the pawn of the gods, it is because
they know me so well, not because
they make my mind up for me."*

Teleus reminds the king of a lesson all Thieves must learn: you can do anything you want, not everything.

Wineshop
⟩⟨⟨⟩

The Vine and the Cup was a reputable establishment, its wine served unwatered, its patrons honest, or mostly so. Nonetheless, conversation quieted at the sound of marching footsteps approaching its door; it was early for the city guard to be out patrolling for drunks. When the marching feet stopped just outside, conversation died away entirely and the room was otherwise silent as men in uniform clattered down the steps from the street. Not the city guard, these were the soldiers of the royal guard, gleaming breastplates and buckles, short swords at their waist, led by the captain himself. The crests of their helmets brushed the low ceiling.

Honest or not, those close enough to do so slipped through the doorway to the kitchens and out the back of the establishment. The rest of the room could only watch as Teleus approached a table in the corner where a young man sat alone, nursing the wine cup in front of him with one hand. The young man's visits were infrequent, but he was known to many of the regulars and they thought even the captain of the guard might approach him with a little more care. He was wickedly dangerous with the hook on the end of one arm and they held their breaths.

"Your Majesty," said Teleus.

Gudix behind the bar leaned forward, thinking he'd misheard. Merinus sitting only a few feet away rocked back, knowing that he hadn't.

Letting the cloak slide from his shoulders, the King of Attolia rose to his feet.

Sitting in Teleus's private quarters, Relius put his cup down with a thump. He looked at his friend in disbelief. "You didn't."

"I did. He has no business going into town with no guard," Teleus said, sounding truculent even to himself.

"You walked into the wineshop with a squad and called him by name?"

"I said, 'Your Majesty.' I'm not calling him by name—he's the king even if he refuses to act like it."

"And he . . ."

Teleus began to look less confident. "He was wearing cloth of gold under his cloak. Looked like a statue of one of the old gods come to life. The entire shop dropped to its knees—mind you, knocking every single stool and bench over in the process. After that, you could have heard a mouse fart. We stood there like the twice-cursed stone pillars of Sia listening to Gudix behind the bar"—Teleus waved his wine cup—"trying to shuffle down to the end of it so he could still see."

Relius shook his head. "Pour me more wine."

Teleus went to fetch the amphora. "He has no business—"

Relius held up his hand. "I know. He has no business. But obviously he didn't need to worry about being stabbed to death in that wineshop, did he?"

Teleus tilted the amphora over his own wine cup as well and grudgingly admitted that Relius was correct.

"I apologized," he said.

"Well, I am sure he appreciated the wonder of that."

"He said never mind, handed me this." Teleus slid a solid

gold coin onto the table. It was a double stater. All on its own, it would have bought any of the finest homes in the city. It was an outrageous sum and Teleus clearly had no idea what it meant.

"Oh," said Relius.

"Oh, what. Is that my severance pay? Do I go back to Pomea now?"

"You could buy a small estate in the country with that, certainly, but I don't think that's what he was suggesting." Relius flipped the coin over, turning the Lily side down and the heads side up. "It's quite a good likeness, really."

Teleus stared down at the king of Attolia.

"He did insist on putting it on the double staters first. I don't imagine many will be minted, but still. The other coins will be coming."

Teleus considered the gold piece. He nudged it with one meaty finger. "It was something of a last hurrah, then."

"I would say that it is unlikely that a most private young man . . . will be hiding out in plain sight ever again."

"I probably owe him a better apology."

"Probably," said Relius.

Teleus sighed.

·☙ EDDIS'S EARRINGS ·❧

(The Palace of Attolia. Throne Room. Gen and Eddis
stand near the wall while dancers pass by.)

EDDIS: Are those my earrings
your wife is wearing?

> GEN: I told you—yours
> were garnets. Those
> [gestures] are rubies. And I
> paid for them.

EDDIS: Really? Where did
you get the money for rubies?

> GEN: Among other things,
> I sold your garnets.

⟩· THE PORTLAND VASE ·⟨

The Portland Vase is a good example of the difference between a real object and the fictional object it inspires. While the technique that made them stayed the same, one large vase became two beautiful wineglasses used to serve remchik in *A Conspiracy of Kings*.

The cameo glass vase is displayed in the British Museum. It was created sometime around the beginning of the Christian era by taking a bubble of one kind of glass and dipping it into another to make a white coating. Once the piece had cooled, the surface was carefully carved to leave figures in white against a blue background.

Melheret knows all too well that appearances can be deceiving.

Envoy

Melheret stood at the rail and watched the capital of Attolia disappear behind the bulk of the offshore island that sheltered it. The emperor had recalled his diplomats from Attolia and Melheret was not looking forward to his homecoming.

The imperial fleet should have been moved, no matter how adamantly the emperor's nephew had insisted that his slave could not know its location. Melheret had said as much, as delicately as he could, knowing he risked offending people far more powerful than he was. Ignorant, narrow-minded counselors had disagreed, arguing that the allied navy was too small to be a threat, and the Emperor was nearing the end of any need for secrecy. Melheret had been right, and they had been wrong, and that was far more dangerous to Melheret than the reverse.

His sense of foreboding only increased as his secretary approached and he held up a hand to caution the man, but it was a hopeless gesture. Ansel blurted out his news for all the sailors around them to hear.

"The figurine of Prokip by Sudesh is gone. Forgive me, Ambassador."

"How?" asked Melheret, surprised by his own calm.

"I did just as you instructed, sir. I checked its case this morning, I locked it, sir, I know I did. I did not take my eyes off it today, I swear, not once did I look away."

"And yet you tell me it is gone."

"I do not know how it could have happened. I just opened the case and found this." He handed over a message with the ambassador's name written on it in the king's hand, familiar to them both.

The ambassador didn't have to open it to know what

it held, but he did anyway. It was a thoroughly civil note wishing him a safe journey home and a reminder that he was always welcome to return. An invitation so warm and so damning it would mean his death if the emperor ever heard of it. It wasn't on paper. The king had written on thick parchment, deliberately, the ambassador was sure. It didn't tear easily. He had to wrench it to pieces, growing angrier and angrier with every effort, until he could feel his face suffused with blood and hear himself snarling as he finally gave up and threw all of the pieces over the ship's rail.

Ansel had backed away in alarm. "Forgive me," he said again and again from a safe distance.

"Oh, shut up," said the ambassador wearily. "You're a free man, I can't throw you over the side, too." There was no point in blaming the secretary for the theft. Melheret would have sworn on his life that the figurine had been impossible to steal—locked in a case and the case guarded every minute, but the king of Attolia was still the thief of Eddis.

"You could have waited until I came belowdecks to tell me," said the ambassador. He looked around at the crowded deck where sailors hastily went back to their work and the other passengers went on pretending to watch the slowly receding shore.

It was Melheret's unfortunate task to persuade his emperor that the king of Attolia was a threat. The sinking of the Imperial fleet should have been evidence enough, but

Melheret knew that men far more powerful than he were scrambling to convince the emperor that the catastrophe had been an accident, a fluke, entirely unpredictable and no fault of theirs. Certainly it could not be the result of Eugenides's careful plans. The Attolian king's intelligence, his ruthlessness, his cunning were going to be obscured by distance and no matter how much the ambassador tried to convince them that the new king of Attolia was dangerous, the Imperial Court was only going to hear that he was an irresponsible fool who stole the ambassador's statue.

"Never mind," sighed Melheret. "Never mind. Go away."

The servant retired belowdecks to the Ambassador's cabin where he locked the door and opened the case that held the statue of Prokip. It was a lovely thing, the god at once graceful and strong, stern but kind. Even the ragged edge where the hand had been broken off to appease the gods did not really mar its beauty. Ansel opened the porthole. It was a shame, really, but the Attolian king paid well and he was a dangerous man to cross. Ansel dropped the statue into the sea.

Even I do not always understand mortals.

The Cook and the King of Attolia

Deep into the dog watches of the night, the king sat hunched at his writing desk reading reports, head propped on his hand. Each time he shifted a page, his hook sank through the paper, scoring the wood underneath with a delicate scratching sound audible in the otherwise quiet room.

He'd had no rest that day, and none the night before. Petrus had shooed him away from the queen's bedside just as the dawn crept up from the east to color the sky. Instead of heading for his own bed, the king had gone to reassure his frightened barons. After that, there had been an audience with the escaped slave Kamet, newly arrived in Attolia, and after that more meetings, including one with the very testy Mede ambassador, who had demanded that Kamet be surrendered immediately. Once he had dismissed both the demands and the ambassador, the king had gone back to the queen's bedside to sit with her until she fell asleep.

"Your Majesty." Hilarion, about to suggest the king get some rest, got such a look he changed his mind. "Perhaps some food?"

The king shook his head. "Has Relius sent no message on from his contact at Meropis?"

"No, Your Majesty." If Relius had sent a message, they all would have known it.

Rubbing his eyes, the king appeared to change his mind. "I do want something from the kitchen," he said.

Ready to do anything that would relieve the awful helplessness he felt, Philologos leapt to his feet. "Perhaps some bread and cheese, Your Majesty? Or some soup?"

"No." The king had already made up his mind. "Some of the spiced almonds the cook makes for altar days."

Philo's heart visibly sank.

"I'll go," said Hilarion. Quite noble of him, thought Lamion.

"No, it's my turn," Philologos insisted. "I'll go."

"Gods, no, I'll fetch them myself," said the king. "Better than waiting for you to wake the cook so she can tell you there are no nuts and you can come back empty-handed to ask if I'd like bread and sausages instead, which will turn out to be also sadly unavailable."

Philo blushed a fiery red. The spiced almonds the king was asking for were prepared once a month to the cook's secret recipe. There was no chance she would give up even a handful of them, and no one in the kitchen would give them out behind her back.

There was no more sand in the king's food. Every meal he ate with the queen was meticulously presented, but outside of that, Brinna, the head of the kitchen, continued to stymie the king's every request. If an attendant was sent for an almond cake, there would be none. If he went to get bread, he would be told it had burned, take yesterday's stale roll instead. If the king asked for coffee, they had to wait an hour for a fresh pot to be brewed, and if they did successfully pry some edible thing away from her, the cook insisted that whatever it was, it was just the thing she had meant to serve that evening, or meant to send to the queen, who she strongly felt deserved it more, or it was something reserved for some special occasion. Brinna would seize the fabric of a man's sleeve to hold him in place while she complained and, Patronoi though he might be, he dared not pull away. No one offends a cook.

"I'll go," said Ion, throwing himself into the breach, only to have the king wave away his sacrifice.

"The last time you went, she told you they didn't have figs, Ion. Figs. Every day they have to send someone out to the garden to clear them off the paths."

"She said she'd just made them all into jam."

"And when I said I'd like some of the jam?"

"She told me the entire batch had stuck to the bottom of the pot."

"Indeed," said the king, getting to his feet. "It's time to put an end to this."

The king was exhausted. The queen was ill. The whole palace was mad with worry. It was emphatically not the time for this.

Nevertheless they all went, the king leading the way with a lantern as most of the lamps in the hallways had already burned down. His guards kept trying to get ahead of him, clutching their short swords in one hand and their long-barreled guns in the other, as if assassins might leap out of any cross corridor. The king moved down the passageway artlessly drifting from one side to the other and there was no way to get by. The attendants trailed farther behind, remembering a time when they would have been pleased to see the king and his cook go at it hammer and tongs.

As they approached the kitchens, the king turned to shine the lantern light on their faces and say in a hushed voice, "There's no need to wake everyone by thundering in like elephants."

How considerate, thought Philo.

How ridiculous, thought Ion. If the king thought he could fetch those almonds away without waking Brinna, he was in for a surprise. She kept them in a jar in a locked cabinet, and that night she'd be dozing in the chair beside that cabinet, ready to leap up if the queen's attendants sent for food or drink.

After squeezing the shutter on the lantern down to a pin-prick, the king handed it to Hilarion. Then he held a finger to his lips and entered the dark kitchen. The banked fires leaked just enough light to navigate between the heavy tables. As Hilarion followed after him, he remembered it was under those tables that the youngest kitchen workers slept, unfortunately only after his foot came down on something soft. There was a squeak that might have been a mouse if it hadn't been followed by some very robust, if high-pitched, curses.

"For gods' sake, Hilarion, we are trying to be quiet here. Could you not—" The king broke off with a shout of pain. Guns clattered to the stone floor. Someone was shouting. Then *many* people were shouting and the king was bellowing something Hilarion finally understood was "Open the lantern, you fool!" So he did.

And there was the king, head awkwardly pulled to one side, his left ear in the pincer grip of the pastry chef herself, both of them only a hair's breadth from the naked blades of the palace guard. Brinna went almost as white as her baking flour. She let go of the king's ear and clutched at her heart instead.

Using his hook to bat the swords away, the king encircled the expansive waist of the cook with the other arm, even as his foot was drawing her chair closer to receive her as he gently lowered her down. He already had her key ring in his hand, a hundred keys of all sizes jangling together, except the very small, delicately made one he'd singled out.

"Zerchus," he said as he handed it off to one of the cooks, "fetch some of the aqua vitae." Without even looking at the guards, he said, "Put those damned swords away," and shamefaced, they did as they were told.

By this time, everyone in the kitchen was awake and crowding around. Those in the back had climbed onto the tables to see. Brinna, tipped back in her chair, was the center of attention. She was trying to call Zerchus back, but he'd already hurried away.

"My key," Brinna gasped. "My aqua vitae."

"*My* key," the king countered. "*My* aqua vitae. Remember?" He was watching her face closely. "'I am the king of the castle. I am the lord of the land. Everything here is mine and everyone mine to command.'"

"If you hadn't chanted that every time you stole a pastry, you wouldn't have been smacked so often for stealing pastries." That was Tarra, one of the jam makers, with a wet cloth for Brinna to hold to her face. She wasn't overawed by the king of Attolia. The king rewarded her lack of deference with a smile.

When Zerchus came back with the aqua vitae, the king took the bottle and demonstrated that he could pour his own drinks, tucking it under his arm and holding the cup Tarra had given him in his hand. Brinna grumbled but emptied the cup. Her breath evened out. The king waited patiently.

"Wretch," she said, when she'd got her breath at last.

"*Handsome* wretch, I think you mean."

"I do not," she said angrily, but her expression softened. "Foolish wretch," she added. She was looking at the hook, perhaps remembering when he was just one of the many errand boys in the palace playing king of the hill on the compost heap in the kitchen garden. Small but scrappy, he'd been almost impossible to dislodge, and had boasted of his success everywhere he went. None of them had ever wondered at the way he seemed to appear and disappear at will.

"We all thought you were just hiding somewhere dodging work, or that you'd run off home again and that sooner or later they'd bring you back."

"Well, I was running off home, and see, I did come back. And I am the king of the castle, aren't I?"

"Hush," said Brinna, "It's not the king who rules this castle."

Sotis gaped at her nerve. The king laughed.

"How is she?" asked Brinna abruptly.

"Better," said the king softly.

"We heard. Didn't know if it was true."

"Petrus says she will live and be well."

"And you came to tell me yourself," said Brinna, gratified.

"No," said the king, shaking his head. "I came for *spiced almonds*. It's not my fault Hilarion is an oaf."

"Oh, that's the only reason the nobodies in the kitchen finally get a glimpse of the great king?"

"Exactly," said Eugenides.

Brinna shook her head in disgust. "You should have come sooner," she said.

"You put sand in my food."

Brinna shrugged. "Didn't know it was you."

"Yes, you did," said the king.

"Not at first," Zerchus protested from behind him and the king turned to glare in his direction before turning back to Brinna.

"You knew."

"You should have come sooner."

"I got rid of Onarkus."

No one in the kitchen had felt the least bit sorry when Onarkus had been blamed for bad behavior in his kitchen and dismissed.

"I suppose that's all right then," said Brinna, mollified.

"Then we can have spiced nuts all around."

Zerchus looked to Brinna, and the king pretended to be outraged.

"Am I king?" he said.

"Not here you're not," said his cook, but she nodded to Zerchus, who pulled the large ceramic jar from its cabinet. After prying off the cork top, he distributed the sweets by the handful.

It was only the beginning of a midnight feast. The king suggested other delicacies, and Brinna agreed to every one. Out came the almond cakes, the cinnamon-swirled pastries, and the curd tarts from cold storage. The kitchen workers, the attendants, and the guards mingled together, all of them eating their fill. Someone heated the pokers in the bank fires to make hot drinks and passed them around.

"What *does* bring you to my kitchen tonight?" Brinna asked.

"Kamet is here," the king told her, dispensing with pretense. "I wasn't sure you'd heard."

"The slave they say Costis brought from the empire? That's Nahuseresh's Kamet?"

"He's his own Kamet now. Still, he may need some help settling in."

"He should come to us then," said Brinna. "And quicker than you did."

"He may also be unsure of his reception."

"We made him welcome before, we'll do so again. Don't you worry, I won't pinch his ear."

"We will send him your way then," said the king. He yawned and stretched. "Before I go, I want some of those almonds."

Hilarion looked for Eryx, who was still holding the jar. Shaking his head sympathetically, the cook slowly turned it upside down. All around him, the kitchen staff, with their cheeks filled like squirrels, stood watching. Brinna patted the king's hand.

"Tomorrow," she said, "I'll make a whole jar just for you."

"Unkingly in so many ways, My King."

﹥･ BRINNA'S ALMOND CAKES ･﹤

This is a Whalen family recipe for a dense, slightly chewy cake baked in an 8" or 9" Bundt pan. For individual cakes, we use a pan for six mini Bundts, or one for six muffin tops. If you don't have a Bundt pan, a 9 x 5 loaf pan will work, too. It's the muffin tops that come closest to the image I have in my mind of Brinna's cakes. My own version of the recipe was copied into a blank book when I was eleven. It appears to have been set down by a semiliterate cook many hundreds of years ago, but my baker friend Sharyn November has standardized and updated it for you.

INGREDIENTS

1½ cup (192g) cake flour

1 cup (112g) almond flour (or ground almonds)

½ teaspoon baking soda

½ teaspoon salt

1⅓ cup (260g) granulated sugar

¾ cup room temperature butter (1 ½ stick, or 170g)

4 eggs

1 cup (240g) sour cream

1 teaspoon vanilla extract

2 teaspoons almond extract

Powdered sugar

METHOD

1. Grease and flour the pan. (Note: Bundt pans are tricky, so make sure to *thoroughly* grease and flour.)

2. Preheat oven to 350°F.

3. In a small bowl, sift together cake flour, almond flour, baking soda, and salt.

4. In a large bowl, cream the butter and sugar together until smooth.

5. Add eggs one at a time to creamed butter and sugar—incorporate each egg into the mixture before adding the next.

6. Add sifted ingredients to butter, sugar, and eggs, alternating them with the sour cream, vanilla extract, and almond extract.

7. Pour batter into prepared Bundt or mini Bundt pans.

8. Bake large Bundt for an hour, or until a deep golden brown and a toothpick inserted in the cake comes out clean.

9. Cool in pan for an hour, then turn out onto rack to fully cool.

10. If desired, sprinkle with powdered sugar before serving.

NOTE

Well-wrapped, this cake will last on the counter for a few days. Do not freeze.

*Dear little chicks, not even fully fledged
and look how resourceful!*

Ina and Eurydice Borrow a Beehive

(in the gardens of the Villa Brimedius)

DIDI: Remember,
we have to ask first.

INA: That's silly.

DIDI: It's not silly!

INA: Shhh! I'll ask, if you
want me to. [Kneels beside
the stack of clay pipes.] Your
Majesty, we are prisoners
here and would borrow your
soldier bees to help us escape.
May we take them?

DIDI: See, a bee
came to my hand!

INA: Well, there's your answer.
Now stand back.

DIDI: We've never used
the whole hive before.

INA: *Don't* let it bump.

DIDI: Ina?

INA: Yes?

DIDI: It's not really
borrowing, is it? If
we're going to smash
the hive on the floor
of the guardroom?

INA: Not all the bees will
sting. The ones that don't
will swarm outside and
start a new hive, maybe a
wild hive in the forest.

DIDI [whispers to the bees.]:
Thank you for helping us.
I hope you can escape, too.

Pheris, I will guide your pen, but you must pray to my sister to inspire your music.

Music to Delight the Ear

I remember that we had finished reading a long and very boring description of the death of the King of the Bructs when Relius rewarded me for my efforts by reaching back to the shelf behind him for the wooden flutes that rested there. Picking up both, he laid one of them on the table and lifted the other to blow a few experimental notes, only enough to show how the sound changed when one of the holes bored in the wooden pipe was covered.

"I cannot play anymore," he admitted. "I have thought it might be possible to make a new flute, one that could be played with my remaining fingers, but it is too much trouble." He shrugged. "See what you can produce."

After I had managed to make a few breathy notes, twiddling one finger up and down, he took the flute away again. I pulled a sad face, and he shook his head. "I am going to teach you to read music."

I could not guess how one might read a sound in the air,

but Relius explained how the notes might be transcribed on a staff, introducing me to the concept of scale and hexachord.

"This notation was developed in Ferria's court several hundred years ago and is now used all over the continent. I do not know if you can cover the stops with your fingers, or control the air with your tongue. It hardly matters. You should understand how music is created even if you cannot make your own." He handed me the plainer flute, saying I might take it with me to see what I could learn from it. "Your uncle Dite rather famously wrote a song using only three notes."

I hurried through the king's waiting room, which was foolish, as I caught Xikander's eye. He insisted I show him what I was hiding, but when he reached for the flute I held it back, looking to Ion for a rescue. When Ion waved Xikander off, I hustled past as quickly as I could, headed for the privacy of my closet. While the racks of the king's clothes and the dummies that held his coats still filled most of the space, some of the chests had been moved out. I had a low bed as well as a stool where I could sit, concentrating all my attention on my new treasure as the morning passed.

"ENOUGH!" shouted Hilarion from the doorway, and I almost dropped the flute. "Are we all deaf, that you think we can't hear you playing the same notes all afternoon? Are we pigeons, that we are supposed to flock to you in delight? No, we are not. We are not pigeons, and if you don't take that flute out to the garden, I will break it over your head."

I smiled, utterly delighted. I knew Hilarion too well to be frightened by his shouting, and I had indeed been trying to produce the coo of the pigeon on my new instrument. I had not thought how the sound might carry through the apartments, where there were few solid doors and most rooms were closed off only by curtains.

I clutched the flute tight to my chest and squeezed past Hilarion, very much indebted to him for his warning. I might have gone to ground in one of my usual hiding places in the garden and given away its location to anyone listening. Instead, I headed to the orangerie, and sat on a bench trying to play the scale Relius had showed me.

I did no more than amuse myself with the flute, though I did pay more attention to the music that was played in court after that. Relius had me copy out notes and rhythms to be sure I understood their transcription. It was quite a few years later when my uncle returned from Ferria that I furthered my musical education.

My uncle brought Juridius to see our mother. I hardly knew my brother, he had changed so much. We had become strangers to each other, and he was very standoffish at first. We have grown more amiable over the years, though never as close as we once were. My uncle Dite, on the other hand, was attentive from the first moment we met. It was he who sat in the music room with me for hours, one of the great harps in between us, as he taught me all he knew. It was he who encouraged me to write down my own songs. I will not forget the first time I heard my music played, nor how proud it made him to hear it.

·࿐· LAMASSU ·࿐·

The first time I saw one of the enormous stone statues of a winged bull, or lamassu, I was a student at the University of Chicago, visiting its museum of antiquities. The lamassu were Assyrian protective deities. Assyria existed in different forms, from city-state to empire, from the twenty-first century BCE to the seventh century BCE. From the early Bronze to the Late Iron Age, they produced many of these giant sculptures and placed them in the gateways of palaces. I have since seen them in museums in London, Paris, New York City, and Berlin.

In the British Museum, I overheard a passing tour guide talking about the lamassu in connection with the Royal Game of Ur. The museum had been cleaning one of its statues and had found an outline of the game board scratched in the stone platform underneath it. The museum contacted other museums, and quite a few game boards were found. The guards may have kept the pieces in their pockets and passed the long quiet hours of their watches playing against each other.

I always check for a game board whenever I see a lamassu, and I remembered those guards, when I was writing *Thick as Thieves*. In the Mede city of Traba, Costis finds that guards and their games are pretty much the same the world over.

⊱· THE ROYAL GAME OF UR ·⊰

The British archeologist Sir Leonard Woolley found five of these game boards while excavating the Royal Cemetery of Ur in the 1920s. Similar game boards were later found in many excavations. No one knew how to play the game, until the 1980s, when a curator at the British Museum was deciphering the cuneiform on a clay tablet. The tablet had

been created in about 177 BCE by a Babylonian scribe, Itti-Marduk-balāṭu. It described how the Royal Game of Ur was played, based on an earlier work by another scribe, Iddin-Bel. Itti-Marduk-balāṭu's tablet had been found in the ruins of Babylon in the 1880s and sold to the British Museum, where it sat unread until Irving Finkel translated it a hundred years later.

Appearances can be deceiving, indeed.
Melheret did not know it was I who brought to
him the missive sent by the next Emperor of
the Mede.

Melheret's Earrings

Melheret was staring into space, picking over his memories like a slave sorting beans, trying to pinpoint the moment he had realized that the king of Attolia was not just a menace, but a potentially lethal one. It might have been after the exhibition match, when he had soundly defeated the king . . . only to suspect afterward that the glee of the onlookers had been directed not at Eugenides, but at him. There had been some secret joke. He hadn't caught it—still didn't know what it was—though he had long since guessed that the king's outrage and humiliation had been an act.

Melheret should have known even before then, though. He should have recognized the danger when the king insisted on a formal introduction every time they met, forcing his sullen attendants to recite the diplomatic courtesies again and again, always with the pretense of never having heard them before, always with that same look of gleeful idiocy on his face. Beyond petty, beyond tedious, it was ridiculous. What kind of a king makes a mockery of himself? Melheret wished he'd seen the answer sooner, but he was a military man, not a diplomat by training. Only a king who was very sure of himself could afford to be laughed at. A king that sure of himself, with Attolia and Eddis and Sounis by his side, all of them hardened by years at war? That king could bring down an empire.

At a whisper of sound, he turned. His wife was standing in the doorway behind him. Her eyebrows had no doubt been lifted when she had first arrived, curious to know what messenger had come to him through the doors of his study, open to the terrace, and not through the main house. That sign of lighthearted inquiry would have faded as he continued to stare into the middle distance, rubbing a finger across his lower lip. By the time he looked up, her expression was carefully composed, hiding her anxiety.

"The Peninsular army routed ours at the Leonyla," he explained. "The emperor's armies have scattered across Roa and are retreating in disarray."

"Is it time to sell my earrings?" She came to sit beside him, speaking as lightly as if she were pawning her jewelry to pay a minor gambling debt.

She wore the earrings every day, told her friends it was because they were a gift from him after his long absence. Their poorly worked pot-silver settings drew no attention, yet they were the most valuable things they owned. The flawless rubies in the settings would be easy to sell if Melheret and his family needed to leave their home on short notice. Precious enough to pay their way out of the emperor's reach.

When Melheret had returned from Attolia and seen his warnings falling on deaf ears, he had only just barely arranged to be sent from the court in disgrace, an effort to distance himself from the oncoming debacles. For him, internal exile was no hardship; on the contrary. He loved the country and would have happily lived out his days on his family's small estate—or would have without the ever-present fear that everything could still be much, much worse.

His wife assumed one of Melheret's few friends at court had sent a warning, but she was mistaken.

"We have had a visit from an imperial messenger—sent by no less than the heir to the empire himself," Melheret told her. "He now believes that my assessment of the Attolians was correct, and he wants me to return to the court."

"Will you?"

"I must."

"And if he is only summoning you to see you executed for the crime of being right?"

He covered her hand with his. "The emperor is old—the empire teeters. It is the heir who must put it right, and to do that, he needs to know just how dangerous the Attolians can be. Only I can persuade him to leave the Little Peninsula well alone."

"I will see about packing our things, then."

"Only my things, dearest."

"But the earrings—what reason will you have to keep them close if I am not with you to wear them?"

"No reason."

"She gave them to you so that you could escape if—"

"No," Melheret interrupted. Cupping his hands around her face, laying his brow against hers, he said quietly, "She gave them to me so you could escape."

"Then I do not want them!" She was weeping now. "I've never liked them. They make my ears ache. We will have them reset into matched thumb rings, and you can wear them on your toes."

He wiped a tear from her cheek. "The emperor must abandon any attempts to control the Little Peninsula. If he does not, the empire may fall. Therefore I must do everything in my power to convince him of the danger, and I will only be able to do that because I will know that you are safe. That is why she gave me the earrings. That was the queen of Attolia's gift to me. I will not forget it."

Remember Kamet who has brought you to your long journey's end. You have all you need from him now.

The Arrival

The villa was built in the old style, built before the first invaders came to the Little Peninsula, its generous courtyard filled with a garden and water reservoirs, cool even when the afternoon sun beat down. The woman who approached the porter at its gates had walked the miles of dusty roads from the capital. To the porter's discerning eye, she carried herself well and may have been quite beautiful once. Still, when she asked to see the Kingnamer, he made her wait in the heat while he went inside to seek instructions.

Kamet wasn't home. It was a woman, very pregnant, who came back with the porter and invited her inside, to the kitchen, not the living room, not the cool seats set out under the eaves of the courtyard breezeways. She was offered a place on a bench, given water and some bread and cheese, and left to rest. From there, she tried to understand the bustle of the large household.

She'd thought the woman at the door had been in charge of the house, but there were two more women she heard the cook call mistress. The children—and there were many children, of all different ages, from toddlers on the floor to young men in their teens—seemed to call all three Aunty. One refilled her cup of water with a smile; another brought her some grapes, equally at ease. Only the pregnant woman eyed her with suspicion.

When Kamet arrived home the porter warned him there was a visitor, a foreigner. Still, he was taken by surprise.

"Laela," he said.

The River Knows

Mother why does the River not rise

It is not the River's time

Why does the seed not sprout

It is not the seed's time

Why does the rain not fall

The leaf not unfurl itself

Where is the hind and why does she not graze the fields before us

It is not their time

The River knows its time

The seed knows its time

The rain the leaf and the hind

They know their time

The River will rise

The seed will sprout

The rains come down

And the leaves unfurl

The hind will bring her children to graze before us

All in their time

*Oh, so wise now, Gen, and still so foolish, so
afraid that she cannot love you as you love her.
Did you not save her? Did she not save you?*

Alyta's Missing Earring

"Eugenides," said one of the Fates.

"What?"

"We know you are lurking. What are you up to?"

"Nothing," said the god of thieves. Then he shrugged. "Hiding."

"From whom this time?"

"Alyta."

All three Fates lifted their heads in surprise. Alyta, though the daughter of the storm god, was one of the gentler goddesses.

"She wants a favor," said the god of thieves.

Sphea, the spinner, nodded in understanding. The gods and goddesses often came to the half-bred mortal son of the Earth, asking him to use the gifts given to him by the Great Goddess on their behalf.

"What could Alyta need stolen?" Metiri asked as she

measured out a length of her sister's spinning.

Eugenides waved his hands, as if pestered by gnats. "Whatever it is, I am not stealing it. I already told her that." He drew close to Hega, looking over her shoulder at the pattern on her loom. "I thought there would be more red," he said.

Hega snorted.

While the weaver's fingers were occupied elsewhere on her loom, the god of thieves deftly shifted several of her threads. When Hega moved her fingers back, she felt the change.

"You've made a knot," she complained.

"Just a twist," said Eugenides. "A little one."

"And look, these threads are out of order now. I will have to unweave this whole section, and Sphea's new yarn will have to wait."

"Then let it stay," Eugenides suggested. Whispering in her ear, he said, "It looks better, this. Doesn't it? Say it does."

Hega gave an irritated sigh, but she left the twist in the weave that Eugenides had made. "But no red," she grumbled. "That comes later."

Periphys moved lightly, the leaves dipping at her passing, the occasional spent blossom falling in her wake. She had a specific objective and wandered a little less than usual on her way.

"Sister," she called as she alighted on a terrace overlooking the lower slopes of the Sacred Mountain. "Stop your drizzle, please," said Periphys, unmantling her hair. "I'm all wet from coming up the valley."

Alyta had been soothed by the sound of water dripping from the branches of the conifers that surrounded her home, but she took pleasure in pleasing others; the pattering of droplets eased, and Periphys blew the clouds away. She sat beside Alyta in the weak sunlight.

"You must have heard us calling. So what keeps you home while we are missing you?"

"I did not hear," Alyta said. "I'm sorry. I was lost in my thoughts."

"Thinking what?" probed Periphys, a penetrating if not powerful wind.

"I was wondering if lovers are more trouble than they're worth," said Alyta.

"Cello is," Periphys answered promptly.

"Cello is my favorite," Alyta reminded her. "I love him best."

"Then he should be happy with that," grumbled Periphys, "and not strive so hard to keep you all for himself."

"You're jealous," said Alyta gently.

"He's greedy," said Periphys pettishly.

Alyta didn't argue that. "But a little greediness in one's lover is not a terrible thing," she said. "Not when it gives me pleasure to indulge it."

"Maybe not," said Periphys. "But I see something is the matter. So tell your sister what it is, and I will see if I can help."

Alyta had had many lovers and many children, but had settled on Cello, one of the mountains and the son of the Earth and Sky, as her husband. He had begged her to belong only to him, and she had agreed.

Cello had a friend, Ente, son of the goddess of discord. Angry at losing Cello to his new love, he was determined to ruin their marriage. With that in mind, he had stolen Alyta's earring, one of a set that Cello had given her.

"Ente will wear it," Alyta explained. "And Cello will assume I gave it to him and think I am still taking lovers in spite of my promise."

"Tell him otherwise. Before he even sees Ente."

"I'm sure I could," said Alyta thoughtfully, "but perhaps he would be hurt that I would think he could be so easily deceived."

"Then tell him after he sees Ente."

"But if he is deceived, I might be the one hurt."

"Then he doesn't deserve you," Periphys pointed out.

"But I like him too much to let him go," said Alyta, not disagreeing with her sister, just pointing out other factors to consider. "And I do not see why I or Cello should suffer for something that is Ente's fault."

"Well, if Cello finds out that Ente has lied, it's Ente who will suffer," said Periphys. "He risks all of Cello's love because he will not share any of it." Privately, she thought Ente and Cello rather deserved each other, but she'd never liked Cello. His mountainous form seemed so often to be in her way.

"Ente is too clever to lie outright," said Alyta. "If he's caught, he will only say he found the earring in the woods and meant nothing by wearing it."

"Then you will have to get the earring back," said Periphys. "And you know who will help."

In the tavern, Gen sat drumming his heels on the side of the bench seat underneath him. The dirt floor was uneven, eroded under the table by sweeping, and his feet didn't reach the ground.

His grandfather frowned at the noise and Gen stopped, his shoulders drooping. The tavern was no more than a shed tacked onto the side of a stable, with a bar that ran its length and, across a narrow aisle, a few booths lined up against the outside wall. The food and drink were no reason to visit. The bread on a plate in front of Gen was filled with grit and the wine was sour, but the tavern keeper chatted with the men at the bar, relaying news from distant places, and that was what they'd come for. Gen had knocked his feet against the wood partly in frustration, partly in defeat. More noise would make no difference. He couldn't hear.

Or rather, all he could hear was the men sitting in the booth behind him. They were telling coarse jokes and laughing about something they'd done that they thought very amusing, and they were loud enough to cover all the more important conversation at the bar.

He gathered they'd been sent by their master to steal something from a woman who had rebuffed his advances. Their master meant to wear the earring they'd stolen and pretend the woman, Alyta, had given it to him. The man would have it in his ear, and when Alyta's husband saw it, he would think the man was his wife's lover and be enraged. Drunk and cruel, the men were laughing at the harm their master intended.

Gen felt sorry for the woman. He caught his grandfather's eye and nodded at the men, but the old man shook his head. It was not their business. Their business was the news from Kathodicia. He'd taken the seat opposite Gen so that he could see the faces of the men talking to the tavern keeper and understand their words better. Gen knew he should have picked that side of the table as well and that his grandfather would tell him off for his mistake later.

Still, it was easy, as they rose to leave, to take the earring, lying temptingly close inside the coat pocket of one of the men. None of them noticed, but of course his grandfather did. Once they were outside, he seized Gen by the arm and shook him hard.

"When he sticks his hand in that pocket and finds that earring gone, who will they blame?" he asked. "The tavern keeper on the other side of the bar? The men who stood with their backs to the booths? No. They will blame the strangers sitting behind them, the ones who walked right past the coat hanging on a hook."

He was angry because the men were very likely to chase them and because they'd be remembered as thieves if they came back to that tavern anytime soon.

"And for nothing," Gen's grandfather told him. "Alyta, whoever she is, will not have her earring back, and when her husband notices, he will still think she's given it to her lover."

Gen hadn't thought of that.

"Get yourself into the woods. I will steal one of the horses and pick you up. We cannot afford to linger here."

They rode hard, and Gen's teeth rattled in his head as he held on tight to his grandfather's coat. When they finally slowed to rest the horse, Gen pulled out the earring to look at it. It was surpassingly beautiful. A tiny lapis urn hung on three golden chains from a solid gold ring. It held sprays of miniature flowers, with blossoms made of seed pearls and leaves enameled in yellow and green. The patterning on the urn was so delicate that even Gen's young eyes had difficulty making it out.

"Let me see it," said his grandfather. Reluctantly, Gen held out his palm. His grandfather shook his head. "You can't keep it."

Gen was truculent.

"We steal in the service of our god and in the service of our king. To do otherwise is common theft and as wrong in you as it is in any man."

"We're keeping the horse," Gen pointed out.

"You use the Thief's skills for yourself, and you will lose the favor of our god."

"But I didn't use the skills for myself," Gen protested. He'd used them for Alyta, who'd done nothing to deserve her husband's anger.

"Are you sure?" asked his grandfather. "When you look at that very fine earring, don't you want to keep it?"

"Yes," Gen admitted. He'd never seen anything like it.

His grandfather had set aside his anger by then, and his words were more compelling for it. "Without the god's favor, you will fall," he warned. "And never know what you have lost until you hit the ground."

Gen didn't say anything; he had no interest in a smack that would make his ears ring all day. Shaking his head, the old Thief stopped the horse and shifted in the saddle so he could look his grandson in the eye. "That earring goes on an altar as soon as we reach the city. You can take it to the temple of Alyta. She will be happy to receive it on behalf of her namesake, I am sure."

Embroidered in swirls of silver thread, the fine silk of her pearl-gray shawl lay like a cloud lightly wrapping her shoulders. The deep purple of her gown was the color of the mountains at sunset, its pattern shot through with streaks of silvery blue that widened as they descended until they met together in the skirt that fell to the floor in ripples around her feet.

"Do you know who I am?" the queen asked as she spun gracefully around to show off the costume.

"A goddess," said the king, with a certainty that brought color to her cheeks. "But I don't know which one," he admitted.

It would be the first time in years, since before the war with the Medes, since before she was married, that a traditional midsummer banquet would be held in Attolia's palace, and all over the city, people were planning their costumes. When she had ruled alone, Attolia had dressed as Hephestia, sole head of the pantheon of the Eddisian gods, but with a king by her side, that costume had been put away. She had spent the morning closeted with her attendants, selecting a new one.

"Alyta," said the queen.

"Goddess of the mountain rain?" the king said, a little wary.

"Phresine suggested it—"

"And I get to play her jealous husband?" said the king, remembering days when he had been secretly afraid his world might dissolve like a sugar cone in the rain. "Remind me to have Phresine cast into outer darkness."

"—because I am a descendent of the goddess," said Attolia, ignoring him. "Or am supposed to be, on my mother's side, and you are Eugenides."

He didn't understand. "I am Eugenides," he said, puzzled. "Do I not need a costume? I might like this idea better now."

"No, you go as your god," said Attolia, as if this connection between Alyta and the Thief were clear. The king's face remained blank.

"You do not know the story of Alyta's earring? Phresine told it to me," said the queen.

"Oh, indeed," said the king, loudly enough that the queen's attendants could hear it from where they sat in the waiting room. "Phresine, source of all the edifying stories I have somehow never heard before!"

So Attolia retold it for him. How Alyta's earring was stolen by a troublemaker and how the god of Thieves stole it back for her. How, in return, Alyta had promised him his heart's desire.

"And what was that?" asked the king.

"No one knows," the queen answered. "When anyone asks, the man playing the Thief always refuses to tell."

The king nodded. Attolia reached out and took his hand. "It's a fine idea," he said, without meeting her eye. When he looked up at last, he stood to share the tenderest of kisses. "You are any man's heart's desire," he said.

So a tailor began to work through the night on a suit of soft, silvery-brown moleskin, and while he worked, the king lay awake.

The celebration of the equinox was a celebration of peace and stability, of the stars and planets in their courses, of all things right in the world. It was a time to set aside worries and hard work and revel in the confidence of good things to come, that confidence often expanding into extravagance and socially sanctioned silliness. When the queen descended the grand staircase, dressed as the goddess Alyta, with her king by her side, in a suit not brown, not gray, but somewhere in between, with no crown but thrush feathers woven into a ring on his head, the cheering could be heard by the guards in their places up on the roof walks.

Still, the court knew their mercurial king well, heard the brittleness behind his laugh, saw the distraction behind his smile, and behind their own smiles began checking ledgers for any missteps they might have made. Eugenides mostly observed while his wife ruled, but his observation was as keen as a razor's edge and sometimes as dangerous.

They were not surprised, only unsettled, when he disappeared, as he still could, from a hall filled with people. They looked to their queen, and because she hid her worries far better than her husband did, they were reassured that whatever occupied the king, it was no concern of theirs. The wine flowed, the music played, and the court danced while the king took his invisible paths out of the palace and across the city, revelers passing him in the street too busy with their own entertainment to see anything but another Eugenides, one of a thousand out that night celebrating.

In the temple of Alyta, the king did not approach the altar. He sat instead at the back of the nave, head tipped down, examining his boots as he tapped their toes together, remembering a visit to the temple made many years earlier.

His grandfather had sent him in alone. Gen had stood some time debating with himself as he shifted from foot to foot. He could have hidden the earring in his boot or under his belt; his grandfather would have been none the wiser. Cynical, even at such a young age, he suspected that the earring would make it no closer to the goddess's treasure room than the high priestess's pocket. She would sell it for its gold in the market. Even more than giving up the earring, he hated the idea of its delicate beauty being melted away to nothing but an indistinguishable lump of metal, no matter how precious.

His grandfather's warning had been very clear, and logical as well. "You jump best when you believe in yourself. You believe in yourself because you know you are the Thief. Fail to deliver up to the gods what you know they demand, and you will never be the Thief. Not here." He'd poked him in the chest. "Not here, where it matters most."

At last, with a sigh, Gen had reached up to slip the earring over the edge of the wide, shallow bowl on the altar. He was too short to see, but he heard it slide down the metal surface until it plinked ever so lightly against the other offerings inside.

When he turned to leave, he found he was not alone after all—a figure stood near the entry door, dressed in the flowing robes of Alyta's priestesses. As he approached, she stepped to meet him, stopping him with a hand on his shoulder. She was very tall—he remembered that, but everyone is tall to a child.

"Thank you," she had said. "It was a generous gift." And he had suspected, even then, that the generosity was not in the reluctant release of the earring, but in its theft.

"And in return, you will have your heart's desire, little Thief," she had promised, and bent to kiss his cheek before she'd sent him blinking into the sunlight where, when his eyes cleared, he found his grandfather waiting.

"Took you long enough," the old man said, and they went to sell the horse.

He'd thought he knew his own heart's desire. He wanted to be the Thief of Eddis. When his cousins mocked him, when his father shouted at him, when his grandfather shouted at him, for different reasons, all he wanted was to be the Thief someday. But he'd had other desires since, and he could only wonder which of them had been granted by the goddess.

She'd called him "little Thief" then. He'd been so overwhelmed by the sight of her, he hadn't even noticed. He'd staggered out of the dark temple into the bright day, thinking the spots in front of his eyes had been caused by the sun.

He did not see Moira when she arrived, did not sense her presence until she settled next to him on the bench. "Asking more humble questions, Eugenides?" she teased. Then she relented. "No, I see. You haven't asked because you are so afraid of the answer. Does she really love you? Did she have any choice?" Gentler than she had ever been before, Moira leaned close and spoke quietly in his ear. "Alyta, goddess of the mountain rain, goddess who fills the streams in summer, loves all her children and all who descend from them, and she is ever gentle in their care."

When Eugenides did not respond, she went on. "Ask your-self, Eugenides: why that orange tree? Why that tamarisk bush? She had promised you your heart's desire while a child of hers was alone in the world and unhappy. See, Eugenides," Moira said, holding out a finger from each of her hands and interlinking them. "Only two threads brought together, two threads that touched," she reassured him. "Nothing more than that. And everything else left up to you."

Pheris, my beloved, make your history, live your story. Timris, waste no time in learning from your teacher.

News from the Palace

Pheris sighed with relief as the carriage drew to a halt. Though the work of a master craftsman, its suspension was not enough to cushion his aching bones. He was happy to have a moment to compose himself before the porter came from his alcove to help him climb down from the high seat. By the time the man had retrieved Pheris's stick,

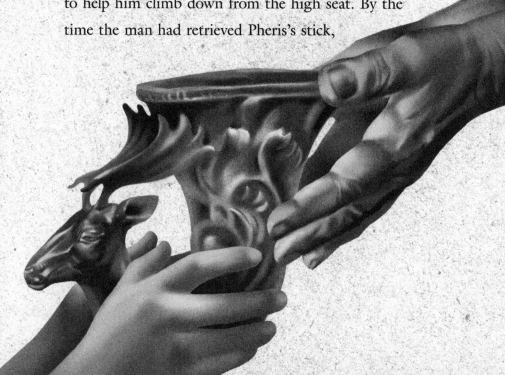

they could both hear the slapping sound of sandals in the garden, the children racing to be first to welcome him to their home.

To his surprise, it was one of the smaller boys who won the race. He must have been playing in the peristyle just inside the main entrance of the villa and had a head start on his siblings, step-siblings, cousins, and more distant relatives.

"Welcome, stranger!" he shouted, skidding to a halt, his face alight with triumph as the other children pattered to a disappointed halt beside him.

Once Pheris had bowed, the triumphant glow dimmed. Unsure of himself, perhaps carried too far by his enthusiasm, the little boy was shifting from foot to foot when Timris, Costis's oldest son, arrived to nudge him sharply between the shoulder blades.

"You welcomed him, you have to fetch the welcome cup."

Everyone turned to the shelf where the heavy pitcher sat, with perilous stacks of cups on either side. The little boy looked up at Timris in mute appeal.

After an audible sigh, Timris said, "I'll pour it for you."

"Not too full!"

"Not too full."

To spill the welcoming wine was bad luck for the house and for the visitor. Timris poured a conservative half cup, accurately judging the little boy's abilities, and even so, every breath was held as the cup was taken in two shaking hands and delivered step by shuffling step.

"As you seek shelter . . . ," prompted Timris.

"As you seek shelter, stranger, find it here. As you seek fellowship, find it here. As you seek peace, find it here, and be no more a stranger in our house."

Pheris shifted his stick briefly to his bad hand, dripped a small libation out onto the stones, and then drained the cup. Once he'd returned it, he shifted the stick back and used his good hand to sign, *Thank you for making me most welcome. Please tell your father and Kamet that I have come to speak to them.*

Perhaps the boy didn't understand. Not until Timris said tactfully, "*All* the papas are out working in the vineyard this afternoon, but we can send a message," did Pheris realize his mistake.

Admiring Timris's diplomacy, Pheris looked back down to the small boy in front of him.

I have confused you with your cousin Philo, haven't I?

The boy tipped his head back, his smile so wide Pheris could see the teeth beginning to fill up the spaces that had been new the last time he'd visited.

This was Phaedon, called Phaedo, the son of Costis's sister and not, as Pheris had thought, Philo, short for Philologos, Timris's half brother. They were the same age and nearly interchangeable, and they loved to be mistaken for each other. Phaedo's father, Dumonius, a better farmer than either Costis or Kamet, ran the estate, but as Timris had guessed, Pheris had not come to discuss farming. He rolled his eyes and signed, as he always did, *Too many children* and everyone laughed. When Timris said, "Phaedo, invite the baron to be comfortable in the peristyle," Pheris lifted a hand to correct him.

Puzzled, Phaedo repeated the unfamiliar sign.

"Secretary," said Timris, aloud, eyes wide. "Baron Orutus has stepped down?"

Pheris nodded. He was the secretary of the archives, newly in charge of all secret communications for Sounis, Eddis, and Attolia. While many at the palace understood him, not all did, and few understood perfectly. Writing out his thoughts took time. He would need someone to be his voice, someone who understood every subtlety in his language. Someone who might follow in his footsteps someday, as he had followed in Relius's. He had not come to tell Kamet and Costis the news; they probably already knew it.

Timris knew why Pheris had come.

⊱· THE QUEEN OF THE NIGHT ·⊰

The Queen of the Night is a fairly recent name for this image in baked clay of a woman with the wings and clawed feet of a bird. The relief was created in Babylonia, probably during the reign of Hammurabi, because it shares some characteristics with the famous stele inscribed with Hammurabi's laws.

No one knows for sure who she is, maybe the goddess Ishtar or Innana or Ereshkigal, or maybe a demon, Lilitu. She takes her name from the iconography in her image— her downward pointed wings are associated with the underworld as the owl's are with night. Along with Grendel's mother from *Beowulf*, the Queen of the Night is the inspiration for the mother of Unse-Sek, the monster of the Isthmus in Kamet's story in *Thick as Thieves*.

Eugenides has had enough of brash young kings and their conquests. He asks Kamet for the story of an old king. Though stories of old kings rarely end well, Kamet knows one that does.

Immakuk and Ennikar and the Gates of Heaven

Great was Immakuk great in years and great in wisdom
    long had he reigned over the land of the Ianna River
    over the people of the great valley
    over the city of copper-topped walls
    shining Ianna-Ir

Long had the city prospered under his rule
    with food in the silos animals in the byres
    gold in the counting houses and
    on the altars of the gods
    offerings of her grateful people

All was well in the city in the valley
    in the land of Immakuk
    where the River rises in its time
    to cover over all the land

to set the seed and then recede

leaving life behind

down from the mountains

floodwaters flow to the land below

gift of the sky god

brought by Ianna

according to the will of Tenep

who orders all

In the fiftieth year of Immakuk's reign

    in that year the River's gift became a curse

The waters rose until they reached across the fields until

      the fields

    and all who dwelled upon them were covered over

    beyond the Ortim markers as far as Pemin-Shuk even farther

    walls crumbled reservoirs were fouled

    dykes and canals dissolved alike in the mud

    and all were drowning man and beast

    disorder visited on Tenep's world

Came his people to Innakar crying Great king

    our farms are drowning our children drowning

    grain in our silos spoilt cows in our byres dead

    great king aid us cried the people

Penemeltip cried the loudest
    wailed and wept and tore his hair
    swore to make any sacrifice
    to appease the gods

Immakuk saw the water lapping
    lapping at the city walls
    saw the waters and despaired
    great in years as well as wisdom
    gray in the beard and gray his vision
    many enemies had he fought
    Unse-Sek had he defeated
    Queen of the Night had he beguiled
    feared he no one Water though
    cannot be injured by the sword
    cannot be beaten by strength alone
    water no army could force into retreat

Immakuk's people said his hero days were past
    Penemeltip loudest of all who condemned him
    the people of Ianna gathered gold to please the gods
    all but Penemeltip of course
    he who cried loudest hid his gold
    when the priests came calling
    gold on gold had Penemeltip
    loved it too much and offered none of it to the gods

Meanwhile Udris black snake of doubt coiled
   in the breast of Immakuk Udris
   coal-black Udris dry and sibilant Udris
   Animate ash of the fire of Beautiful things burned
   Udris slipped through his heart
   dark were Immakuk's thoughts
   deep his fears

To Ennikar Immakuk said
   I am old and my hero years are behind me
   I cannot help my people

To Immakuk Ennikar said
   was not the Queen of the Night against you
   was not the whole land of the dead against you
   when you came for me there
   great you are in years and in wisdom
   great defender of your people I am with you
   drive out Udris drive out the snake of doubt
   set upon this problem
   with the wisdom of your years

So Immakuk set upon this problem with his wisdom
   step by step he descended to the sacred well
   he was purified and step by step climbed to the
   Altars of the gods of Shesmegah and Anet Tenip

the goddess Ianna asked them all what god was against

   his people

there was no answer

long and long thought Immakuk he said

it is no god but Disorder who is our enemy here

Hodus opens and closes the gates of heaven

my friend We know Disorder do we not

from our greener days Ennikar perhaps Hodus sleeps

or dallies said Ennikar

if a man dallies might not a god?

we must ask Hodus to close the gates

Said Ennikar we must bring order back to Tenep's world

Immakuk summoned all his people

   told them to make a great noise

   loud enough to wake Hodus if he slept

   or gain his attention if he was preoccupied

   all the citizens of the city of copper-topped walls

   banged their drums banged their pots their pans

   cried out all their voices together

   and still in the mountains rain fell

   and around the walls of the city

   the waters rose

What will our great king do now to save us?

   cried Penemeltip. The waters rumble still through

the gates of heaven and rain falls in the mountains
the River overtops our dikes and roads

Then if Hodus does not close the gates of heaven we must
said Immakuk we who have been to the underworld
and returned
we will ascend to the heavens.
that is a hero's journey said Ennikar

How will you reach the heavens great king
said Penemeltip naysayer no man can fly
you were a great hero in your time and
returned from the land of the dead
now you are old gray in beard and gray of vision
you cannot see a way to save us
offer nonsense to assuage our fears
no man can carry himself into the sky

No man will ascend the heavens who stands
saying it cannot be done Penemeltip naysayer gold hoarder
I am Immakuk great king and I say I will
ascend the heavens and see the gates of heaven closed.

Immakuk set upon the problem with his wisdom
and with his cunning. He went to Crow
known for his golden feathers proud of his golden feathers

like Penemeltip the crow loved his gold
   loved most of all his golden apples golden as the sun

Immakuk waited until night said to the Crow
   what has become of your golden feathers I see them not
   all feathers lose their color in the night
   trade me some of your golden apples said cunning Immakuk
   I will tell you how you may have your feathers always bright

Crow gave him the apples and Immakuk
   went next to the goddess of the bees to ask her help
   your fields are water covered your bees despair
   of finding their fruitful resting places
   lend me your bees and I will close the gates of heaven
   and the River will recede
   the goddess gave him a pot with a lid sealed on with wax

In the morning as the chariot of the god
   carrying the shining sun
   was on the horizon
   Immakuk melted the wax lifted the lid
   and released the bees

The bees flew up to sting the horses
   the horses kicked against their traces
   Anet's chariot carrying the sun fell off its course

and neared the earth
as the waters all around them steamed

Immakuk's people cried out in fear but Crow was ready
he snatched up the sun even brighter than his apples
snatched up the sun in his beak and flew back into the sky
calling back to Anet now I will carry the shining sun
and my feathers will be always bright

Anet whipped his horses but they were wild still and would
not answer
Anet left his chariot leapt into the sky to follow Crow
chased him all across the sky and all the while
crow's feathers lost their shine ash falling on his head turned it black
ash falling on his wings turned them black

At the end of the day when Crow saw himself reflected
in the water at the edge of the world
he cried out in horror at the color of his feathers cried out in horror
and dropped the sun at last
and that is how Crow got his black hood and wings
you'll hear him still poor hooded Crow cawing about his feathers

Beyond the horizon Anet caught the sun put the sun to bed
came back to find his horses and his golden chariot
gone

Immakuk had bottled up his bees safe in their jar
 and Ennikar approached the horses with soothing sounds
 and golden apples and had his way
 Anet's horses love an apple no less than any horse
 and Ennikar and Immakuk had the chariot of the god
 Immkakuk and Ennikar in the golden chariot
 went to their city
 spoke to their people
 said they would close the gates of heaven
 end the rain in the mountains
 and to Penemeltip who so loved his gold
 they said see here Penemeltip gold hoarder
 the gods know you and have sent you gold
 blessed by the gods the only gold that makes more gold
 and blessed by the gods are you Penemeltip
 as Penemeltip foolish Penemeltip drew near
 Immakuk opened again the jar of the goddess's bees
 the gold that makes more gold indeed
 the bees flew out and chased Penemeltip
 until he threw himself into the River
 and is still there just his nose showing above the water
 near the harbor wall

Then Immakuk and Ennikar took their leave
 said we are great in years and great in wisdom
 our people look to us to save them

we will close the gates of heaven

when the waters recede you will know we have succeeded

if we do not return

you will know we have succeeded

I anoint my son as king

give him my blessing

call him wise and he will grow wiser

a great husband and defender of his people

In the stolen chariot of the god

    they rode around the city

    around the walls of the city

    and leaving his son to rule

    Immakuk rose into the sky

None know what became of Immakuk

    none know what became of Ennikar

    but they know the gates of heaven closed

    the River ceased its rising

    returned to where its banks once were

    and the land washed flat slowly warmed in the sun

    and Tenep's seed was there

    took hold

    and the land was green again

Some say that Immakuk and Ennikar died
    some say that they live still and work the gates
    in Hodus's place. Or wake him if he sleeps
    helping bring order to Tenep's world
    the rains have never been so heavy
    the floods never so deep or so wide
    and just in case Immakuk is sleeping
    or Ennikar dallies
    and the gates need closing

The people of shining Ianna-Ir make noise
    with cymbals and their drums
    shout their names even until this day in the city
    of Ianna-Ir
    the shining city

We are here, beloved, when you take up your burden, and when you lay it down.

The End of Eddis

Eddis opened her eyes in the deepest dark of the night and knew what had woken her, not a noise, or none that mortal ears could catch, but a reverberation in her heart. She threw off her covers, or tried to—she had to slide herself out from underneath them before struggling to her feet.

"Your Majesty?" The sleepy voice of her attendant came from the couch.

"A robe," said Eddis.

The girl sighed—wanted to refuse—but Eddis was queen still and queen in her own right, as her foolish grandson had come to realize. No matter that his ministers had dismissed her warnings—she hadn't needed the Union King's command to rule her Eddisians. She never had.

By late summer, everyone had felt the ground shake under them as the Sacred Mountain kicked ash and rocks into the sky. When the Union King had still refused to order people to safety, Eddis had done so herself, sending her messengers

166

to the scattered villages, the outlying farms, even to the shepherds with their flocks high in the summer pastures. The faithful and the fearful had listened. Packing what they could carry, they had driven their animals ahead of them down from the mountains.

The capital city of Sounis was filled to bursting. The inns were overflowing with people, the streets clogged with sheep and goats. Her grandson had come to complain and she'd laughed, told him his ministers would just have to make the best of it. The Eddisians were his citizens, too.

The corridors of the palace were empty. Trailing after the queen, her attendant was plucking at her sleeve. What was the girl's name? Hedia? Hepita? Eddis couldn't be bothered to remember. She was heading for the stairs to the roof, to see with her eyes what her heart had told her was near.

"Your Majesty, Your Majesty," the girl beseeched, tugging at her arm now, trying to persuade her to return to her chambers, at least to dress if she was going to be out in the night. Eddis took no notice. Who would be awake to see the old queen wearing her nightgown?

Her heart seemed determined to jump out of her chest. Starting up the stairs, she stumbled. Eddis heard a gasp from behind her, and there on the step above was Eugenides, with his familiar smile and his hand held out to her, the trickster. She almost didn't take it, but she didn't want to fall, not yet anyway, and with him to steady her, she continued to climb.

A guard was stationed on the roof walk, someone to see her in her nightgown after all. Eddis hardly cared. Moira was waiting by the parapet and beside her, her mother Periphys, bringing with her the scent of sulfur and ash. Eddis blinked the sting from her eyes and turned toward the Sacred Mountain. With no moon to light it, the smoke, gathered around the peak, was a gray smudge on a black sky, discernible only by the absence of the stars it hid from view.

In the blink of an eye, the cloud lit up from underneath, revealing its immensity. It stretched up toward the highest reaches of the sky, all fiery red and orange. There was no sound at first . . . almost as if the night were holding its breath. Then came the thunderclap—so loud Eddis slapped her hands over her ears as the stones under her feet danced. She would have fallen had Eugenides's arms not been wrapped around her. The mountain roared and the waves of sound rolled through her, setting her heart banging with their rhythm.

The guard was shouting. The palace was shaking itself to pieces. The entire city must have been awakened and probably everyone in it was shouting, but the noise of the mountain drowned out every other sound, except, oddly, the voice of Moira speaking quietly to Hermia, that's what the girl's name was—Hermia.

"No, you don't need to stay. You run along now. She doesn't need you anymore."

Eddis didn't need Hermia, no. She didn't need anything. A great weight was gone, lifted away at last. She was tired, but all was well. Her heart had stopped its terrible thumping and all she felt was a tremendous sense of well-being. She was lying on the stones, though she didn't remember falling.

Far away, molten rock was rolling out from what was left of the Sacred Mountain, sweeping down to obliterate all before it. Filling every valley, streaming rivers of fire were reaching long fingers toward the sea as the sky rained ash and rock and more fire.

"Sleep now," said Moira gently.

Eddis closed her eyes.

Every ending a beginning.

Gitta

Gitta flipped the book closed and sighed heavily. "More books about dead people," she said.

"I'm sorry, Your Highness," said her tutor. "I thought we'd found something you would enjoy."

She waved away his comment and then remembered that was rude and sat on her hands. He looked down to hide a smile.

"I *do* like the story," Gitta insisted. "But everything in it happened hundreds of years ago."

"Not quite that long," he murmured.

"I want something interesting to happen *now*."

"Your sister's wedding is surely interesting." The palace was in near-constant commotion as the day of the ceremony drew near.

Gitta might have snorted. Very delicately. "Hennis's wedding is the . . . the . . . *antithesis* of interesting," she said, borrowing a word from her philosophy primer. "I have to be at every single rehearsal, even though all I am expected to do is stand still. They could make a dummy of me and stuff it in a velvet dress. No one would notice, and even if they *did* notice, no one would care."

"That's not true," said the tutor, his tone gentle but reproving.

The princess glowered but accepted the rebuke. She understood her role and its responsibility, and he knew she would not have expressed her exasperation to anyone else.

Slowly, she traced the pattern tooled in the leather cover of the second volume of the books of the queen's Thief, then slipped it neatly into the stack beside her. "Some of the volumes are missing," she pointed out, reading the numbers on the spines.

"Some have been lost over the years. We know about them from descriptions in other authors' works, so the numbering hasn't been changed." He had, in fact, chosen her reading material well. She had been surprised and delighted by Eugenides the Great, always so dignified in her other history books, behaving so like a rascal in his own. It was the strict and very dull routine of her own life that she chafed against, not her lessons.

"May I look at the map?" she asked, reaching for the parchment. "I don't see why the Mede ambassador wanted Attolia to take Cymorene."

"It was crucial as a supply route for further invasion. From Cymorene, you see, they could move to the Lesser Peninsula. Controlling the Lesser Peninsula, they could threaten the greater one and eventually the rest of the continent."

"Tykus." Gitta pointed to the place on the map where the tutor's name was carefully lettered. "You've spelled your own name wrong."

"No, that's my name," said her tutor. "We say it Tycho, but remember I am named after my great-grandfather." He pointed to a book with a cover that did not match the others. "I hope you will eventually read his book—a history of the first invaders of the Lesser Peninsula, but it's very dry and you should probably wait a year or two."

"I was supposed to be named after Great-Grandmama."

"Indeed," said her tutor.

"Hennis told me there was a big fight when Papa said I had to have a Brael name."

"Her Highness may be exaggerating," the tutor suggested.

"She said Great-Grandmama called Papa a cretin in front of half the meet—"

Her tutor tapped the stack. "Maybe we could look at a few more pages before the next rehearsal for the wedding festivities."

"—and I ended up being named Gittavjøre instead," Gitta finished before she pulled out the next book and obligingly began to read. "Hennis said it's the only time Great-Grandmama ever lost a fight."

At their next lesson, delayed by the wedding and all the events that surrounded it, the princess was very quiet. Tykus was not surprised. He hoped someone had talked to her before the official announcement.

They moved through the various subjects, leaving the history lesson for last, as always. It was her favorite, which kept her motivated through less interesting work and also allowed her to go on reading and asking questions until her attendant said their time was up.

Gitta fingered the books laid out on the table. "You

knew," she said. It was not a question and not quite an accusation.

"There were rumors," he told her.

Her tutor had not chosen the reading just to entertain her.

When the envoy had come north two years earlier, everyone had expected an offer for Hennis, as similar offers had been made in the past for the hand of her mother and her grandmother. Those offers had been seen off with a high hand by her great-grandmother. The old queen remained adamantly against such a match for Hennis, and so the diplomatic visit had seemed pro forma only. The envoy had been presented at court, had taken one look at Gitta, and then to all appearances lost any interest in Hennis.

After six weeks of cordial socializing and several meetings behind closed doors, he'd gone away again without, so far as anyone knew, making any offer at all. Rumor had it that Hennis's nose was out of joint, though she maintained she hadn't wanted the match to begin with. The envoy hadn't appeared disappointed, on the contrary. He'd looked very pleased with himself when he left, and surprisingly, so had the old queen. She'd died only a few weeks afterward, falling asleep in a comfortable chair by the fire and never waking.

There was no official announcement. There could not

be one when Hennis, the older daughter, was not yet engaged, much less married. People had drawn their own conclusions.

Gitta said, her voice low, "You didn't tell me."

"It wasn't my place, Your Highness."

"No," Gitta agreed. "But it could be."

The tutor opened his mouth and closed it again, pinching his lips tight. He knew her well enough to have seen this moment coming; he just hadn't expected it so soon.

While he sat blinking, Gitta waited patiently, with the look in her eye her great-grandmother had seen the day she was born.

The tutor did not get up from his seat, but he lowered his head briefly in respect. "Let me be the first to offer you my service, Your Highness," he said.

Gravely, the princess held out a hand for him to kiss, and they turned back to their books. When they reached the end of the lesson, Gitta stared down at the last page, as if reluctant to see Pheris's story end.

"None of them ever saw the eruption of the Sacred Mountain," she said.

"Eddis did, though she was very old. By then, her grandson was high king and she had warned him, so he ordered the people remaining in the mountains to evacuate."

"Great-Grandmama had already left."

"A long time before that, yes. After her brother disappeared."

"So he never became king and she was never his Thief."

"No," said the tutor. "That is a sad part of the story."

"Did they ever find out what happened to the lost prince?"

"It may be in the missing volumes of Pheris's work. Some sources say he knew, but no one can be certain. We know it was Pheris who helped Eugenia run away."

"I remember. You said that was why they called Pheris the Princess Thief." Gitta laid the book flat and slipped her fingers around the pages. "Now there is no more Eddis, no Sounis, no Attolia."

"They are still there, Your Highness." Tykus tapped the map. "They have just united into Ephestalia, one country with one king and . . . one crown prince."

Gitta wasn't looking at the map. She was gently flexing the pages of the book. Tykus had shown her how a secret picture painted on the edges was revealed when they were bowed just so. Head down, she said, "They wanted Mama to come be their queen and Grandmama too, when they were my age. Hennis told me Great-Grandmother wouldn't allow it."

"That's true."

"Hennis said she must have hated the Attolians."

"We don't know the queen's reasons," said Tykus.

The picture on the edge of the book's pages was a silhouette of the mountains of Eddis, no more than a slice of landscape with the Sacred Mountain rising above the others. It appeared, disappeared, appeared again.

"What else did Her Highness tell you?" Tykus asked gently.

"That they are a backward country and she wouldn't want to be their queen."

The tutor, unsure how much to say, hazarded that Her Highness was very happy with the marriage that her parents had contracted for her.

As he'd hoped, the hint was enough. "She would never admit she wanted to be a queen," said Gitta, but her head was still bent. "Father says that I will go next summer to spend the rest of my engagement with my husband's family, because that is the tradition in the south." She brushed away an unprincesslike tear. "It doesn't snow there, even in winter."

"It does in the mountains."

"I don't speak their language."

"You're learning it very quickly."

"I'm a foreigner, I have different gods, I don't *look* like them. What if they don't like me?" She was thirteen and, princess or not, perilously close to wailing.

"Your Highness," Tykus said calmly, "Remember that your great-aunt Gittavjøre, for whom you were named, was born after her parents had been childless for many years. That's why they chose for her the name they did.

Strictly speaking, it means 'God's gift,' but it is also understood to mean 'well born.' The dowager queen was a very strong-minded woman, and if she gave you that name instead of her own, Eugenia, it was because she knew it would suit you equally well."

"Tycho," Gitta whispered, "Do you think I will be a good queen?"

"Your Highness, I know you will. You will be a great queen."

BRAEL

EPIDI

PENTS

BRAEL

GANTS

SOUTHERN
GANTS

FERRIA

Greater Peninsula

M
E
D
E
E

This map
of Eddis, Attolia,
and Sounis was
prepared for Her
Highness Gitta
kingsdaughter by her
tutor, Tykus Namikus,
for her reference while
reading the books of
the Queen's Thief.

Middl

Hylas

ANAN

Ananite
Highlands

Gulf of Braets
Oncevar
ELENZE
UR
Mûr
Letnos
Salik
Hanaktos
Elisa
SOUNIS
SOUNIS
Irkes Forest
Methona
Matinea
Evisa
Hephestial Mountains
EDDIS
EDDIS
Sacred Mountain
Sea of Olives
Pirrhea
Kahlia
Rhea
Ephrata
Aracthus R.
Leonyla Pass
Stinos
ROA
MAGYAR
Little Peninsula
ATTOLIA
ATTOLIA
Ellid Sea
Cymorene
Sea
Sukir
Shallow Sea
SHENENISH
Zabrisa
Zaboar
ZABOAR
Koadester
Menle
Sherguz
Hemet
HEMSHA
IANNA-IR
MEDE
Traba
Perf
SIDOSIA
PLASSE

"If we truly trust no one, we cannot survive."

SOME PERSONS OF SIGNIFICANCE:
A LIST OF CHARACTERS IN THE QUEEN'S THIEF NOVELS

Agape: Youngest daughter of the Eddisian baron Phoros. She is a cousin to the queen of Eddis and to Eugenides the thief. She is nicer than her sister Hegite.

Aglaia: One of Attolia's attendants.

Akretenesh: The Mede Ambassador to Sounis.

Alenia: A duchess in Eddis who was incensed when Eugenides stole her emerald earrings.

Alyta: A gentle goddess of welcome rain, rain in the distance, and rain in the mountains. She is known for having many lovers and many children, mortal and immortal.

Ambiades: The Magus's apprentice. His grandfather was executed for conspiring against the king of Sounis. Gen calls him Useless the Elder.

Anacritus: An Attolian baron with a wife and a lover. He is a strong supporter of the queen.

Anet: The sky god in the Mede pantheon.

Ansel: Free servant of Melheret, the Mede ambassador to Attolia.

Aracthus: An Eddisian god. Associated with the River Aracthus.

Aristogiton: A friend of Costis and a soldier in the Attolian guard. Costis borrows his name when he needs an alias.

Artadorus: Another baron with a wife and a lover. He's been roped into Baron Erondites's schemes before. At the Baron's suggestion, he misreported the kind of grain he grows in order to pay less in taxes.

Attolia: Irene, queen of Attolia.

Aulus: An Eddisian soldier and minor prince of Eddis enlisted as an ad hoc nanny for the king of Attolia.

✦ ✦ ✦

Benno: A guard hired by Roamanj to accompany his caravan.

Boagus: An Eddisian soldier and babysitter of Eugenides.

Brinna: The head cook in Attolia's kitchens.

✦ ✦ ✦

Caeta: One of Attolia's attendants.

Casartus: Admiral of Attolia's navy.

Cassa: Owner of the honeyed hives in the Mede epic of Immakuk and Ennikar.

Cello: A mountain god. Lover of Alyta.

Chloe: A younger attendant of Attolia.

Cleon of Attolia: One of the king's attendants.

Cleon of Eddis: A dim-witted, but not evil, cousin of Eugenides. Eddis proposed him as an attendant for the high king, but Cleon spectacularly rejected the king's invitation.

Cletus: An Attolian baron, supporter of the queen.

Costis: Costis Ormentiedes, a soldier in the Attolian guard. He is unwillingly embroiled in the politics of the court by Eugenides.

Crodes: A soldier of Eddis. Cousin to the queen and to Eugenides.

✦ ✦ ✦

Death: Lord of the Underworld. Brother of the Queen of the Night.

Dionis: One of Eugenides's attendants.

Diurnes: A member of Costis's squad in the Attolian guard.

Drusis: A new attendant to the king. Motis and Drusis are brothers.

✦ ✦ ✦

Earth: The origin goddess in the Eddisian creation stories.

Eddis: Helen, queen of Eddis.

Efkis: An Attolian baron. Because of Eugenides's schemes, he was thought to have betrayed the queen of Attolia.

Elia: One of the queen of Attolia's attendants.

Enkelis: An ambitious lieutenant in the Attolian guard, briefly promoted to captain by the queen of Attolia.

Ennikar: One of the heroes in the Mede epic of Immakuk and Ennikar.

Ephrata: An Attolian baron.

Erondites: An Attolian baron, one of Attolia's oldest enemies. Father of Erondites the Younger and Sejanus.

Erondites the Younger, called Dite: Baron Erondites's son and one of Attolia's most fervent supporters.

Eugenides: An Eddisian who served as the queen's thief of Eddis before becoming king of Attolia. Also called Gen.

Eugenides: The Eddisians' god of thieves.

✦ ✦ ✦

Galen: Eddis's palace physician.

Ghasnuvidas: Emperor of the Mede. He has been diagnosed with an incurable disease that leaves lesions on the skin, and he has passed over his own sons in order to name his nephew as his heir.

Godekker: An escaped slave living in hiding in Zaboar. He agrees to hide Kamet and Costis.

✦ ✦ ✦

Hamiathes: A mythological king of Eddis. To reward him, he was given Hamiathes's Gift, which conferred immortality and the throne of Eddis.

Hegite: Daughter of the Eddisian baron Phoros. Older sister of Agape.

Heiro: Daughter of one of the barons in the Attolian court. Eugenides dances with her but not with her older sister, Themis.

Hemke: A shepherd on the salt flats of the Mede empire.

Hephestia: The Great Goddess. Head of the Eddisian pantheon. Goddess of volcanoes. She is the daughter of Earth and Sky. They have given her the power of their lightning bolts and earthquakes.

Hespira: In the Eddisian story of Hespira and Horreon, she was lured to the underworld by the goddess Meridite, who wanted her to marry Horreon, Meridite's son.

Hilarion: The oldest of Eugenides's attendants.

Hippias: The Secretary of Attolia's archives until his unexpected death. He was replaced by Orutus.

Horreon: An Eddisian god, the son of the goddess Meridite. He was a blacksmith who made magical armor forged in the fire of the Hephestial Mountain.

Ileia: One of Attolia's senior attendants.

Imenia: One of Attolia's senior attendants.

Immakuk: One of the heroes from the Mede epic of Immakuk and Ennikar.

Ion: One of Eugenides's attendants.

Ion Nomenus: He was the faithless attendant to Sophos when he was held captive by the Mede ambassador Akretenesh and the Sounisian Baron Brimedius.

Iolanthe: One of Attolia's senior attendants.

✦ ✦ ✦

Jeffa: The former secretary of Nahuseresh. When he died, Kamet took his place.

✦ ✦ ✦

Kamet: An enslaved Setran, private secretary to Nahuseresh.

Kepet: A Setran slave dealer in the Mede empire.

Kununigadak the Devourer: A terrifying monster who guards the gates of the underworld in the stories of Immakuk and Ennikar.

✦ ✦ ✦

Lader: A very unpleasant cousin of Eugenides. Deceased.

Laecdomon: A disruptive member of Aristogiton's squad in the Attolian guard and an agent of Baron Erondites.

Laela: A slave in the househould of Nahuseresh. A friend of Kamet's.

Lamion: One of Eugenides's attendants.

Lavia: One of Attolia's attendants.

Legarus: One of the men in Aristogiton's squad in the guard. He is quite beautiful and uses it to what he thinks is his advantage.

Luria: One of Attolia's attendants.

Lyopidus: The mortal brother of the god Eugenides. Jealous of his brother's powers, he asked Eugenides to steal the Sky's lightning bolts and died when they set the world on fire.

✦ ✦ ✦

The magus: One of the king's most powerful advisors; a scholar.

Marin: One of Nahuseresh's dancing girls. He and Kamet were both in love with her.

Marina Erondites Susa: The only daughter of the Baron Erondites, she was disinherited when she married against her father's will.

Medander: One of the king of Attolia's attendants.

Melheret: The Mede ambassador to Attolia.

Meridite: An Eddisian goddess. Mother of armorer Horreon.

Minister of War: Eugenides's father.

Minos: An Attolian baron. Publicly a supporter of the queen.

Miras: One of the new gods of Attolia, god of light and arrows. Worshiped by soldiers.

Moira: Messenger goddess of the Eddisian pantheon and also a record keeper. Her name means *fate*.

Motis: Became an attendant when two of the king's attendants were retired. Motis and Drusis are brothers.

Nahuseresh: The Mede ambassador to Attolia. Nephew of the emperor; younger brother of the heir to the emperor. He attempted to woo the queen of Attolia as a means to her throne and failed.

Neheeled: Nahuseresh's older brother, heir to the Mede Empire.

Ne Malia: Mede goddess of the moon, fertility, and rebirth.

Nine Gods: The main pantheon of the new Attolian gods. They defeated the giants.

Nuri: A Mede god of the river and the flood.

✦ ✦ ✦

Olcthemenes: In the Eddisian stories of the old gods,

Olcthemenes was the tailor who turned a blanket into a suit of clothes for the god Eugenides.

Olmia: In the Eddisian stories of the old gods, Olmia the weaver made a hat from bird feathers for the god Eugenides.

Onarkus: The head of the queen of Attolia's kitchen.

Oneis: A heroic figure from the Epic of Oneis.

The Oracle: Oracle and high priestess at the new temple being built for Hephestia above the palace in Attolia.

Ornon: A minister to the queen of Eddis. Ambassador to Attolia. Subsequently Attolia's ambassador to the Mede empire.

Orutus: Secretary of Attolia's archives, which is to say, her master of spies.

✦ ✦ ✦

Pegistus: Attolia's Minister of War.

Pelles: One of Eugenides's attendants.

Periphys: A goddess, one of the lighter winds.

Permindor of Nilos: Also called Perminder of Sounis, he was proposed by Sophos to be a new attendant to the high king.

Petrus: Attolia's personal physician for years.

Pheris Mostrus Erondites: The nephew of Dite and Sejanus, and the firstborn grandson of Marina, the only daughter of the Baron Erondites. He shares his name with his grandfather who is Erondites.

Philia: One of the goddesses of the Attolian pantheon. She is the goddess of mercy.

Philologos: Youngest but highest ranking of Eugenides's attendants.

Phoros: A baron in Eddis; father of Agape, Hegite, and two other daughters.

Phresine: Oldest of Attolia's attendants.

Piloxides: A general of Attolia's armed forces.

Pol: Captain of Sophos's father's guard; a soldier.

Polemus: A new attendant to the king.

Polyfemus: One of the giants who supposedly built the old walls of Sounis's prison and the roads of Eddis.

Proas: An Eddisian god of green and growing things.

Prokep: A Mede god; a statue of him was made by the sculptor Sudesh.

✦ ✦ ✦

Queen of the Night: Sister of Death and mother of Unse-Sek.

✦ ✦ ✦

Relius: He was the secretary of the Archives, with many, many, lovers; one of whom turned out to be a spy for the Mede Emperor.

Roamanj: A caravan master who hires Costis and Kamet as guards.

✦ ✦ ✦

Sejanus: The youngest child of Baron Erondites.

Senabid: A character in skits, a slave who makes a fool of his master.

Shef: A slave dealer in the Mede Empire.

Shesmegah: In the Mede pantheon, goddess of mercy, forgiveness, and second chances.

Silla: One of the queen of Attolia's attendants.

Sky (god): Created by Earth, he is the second god in the Eddisian pantheon.

Snap: Also called Pepper. Pheris's pony.

Sophos (Useless the Younger): Apprentice of the magus;

future duke; nephew of the king and his heir. He becomes king of Sounis.

Sotis: One of Eugenides's senior attendants.

Sounis: Sophos's uncle and king of Sounis. He had no children of his own. In exchange for his half-brother's support he has named his nephew, Sophos, as his heir.

Stadicos: One of Attolia's barons, corrupted by the Mede ambassador, Nahuseresh.

Stenides: Eugenides's brother, a watchmaker.

Susa: One of Attolia's barons. Devious, but not necessarily an enemy of the queen. He is baron over the lands where Costis's family has their farm.

✦　✦　✦

Teleus: The captain of the Royal Guard. He only has one lover.

Temenus: Gen's brother, a soldier.

Tenep: Usually the most gentle of the gods, she turns her anger on the world when Ennikar steals from her.

Thales: Wrote about the basic elements of the universe; Eugenides was copying his scroll before he went on his mission to Attolia.

Thalia: Costis's younger sister.

Themis: Erondites recruits Themis and hopes to make her the king's mistress, but Eugenides only dances with Themis's younger sister, Heiro.

Therespides: An Eddisian known for his philandering. Also known for selling information to anyone who will pay him.

Timos: Cousin of Eugenides and Eddis. He dies stopping Attolia's advance up the main pass into Eddis.

Titus: Gen's cousin who once broke several of Gen's ribs in a beating.

Trokides: A general of Sounis's armed forces.

✦ ✦ ✦

Ula: Goddess of the hearth and healing.

Unse-Sek: A terrible monster that roamed the isthmus in the stories of Immakuk and Ennikar, child of the Queen of the Night.

✦ ✦ ✦

Verimius: One of the king's attendants. He has a wife and various lovers until he was sent home from the Attolian court.

✦ ✦ ✦

Witch of Urkell: In the Epic of Immakuk and Ennikar, she is Ennikar's lover and the daughter of Ninur.

✦ ✦ ✦

Xanthe: Eddis's most senior attendant.

Xenophon: One of Eddis's generals.

Xikander: One of the king's less pleasant attendants. Poor Gen has so many unpleasant attendants. Xikander and Xikos are brothers.

Xikos: Another one of the king's unpleasant attendants. Xikander and Xikos are brothers.

✦ ✦ ✦

Zerchus: A cook in Attolia's kitchens.

"So many things are obvious in retrospect."

DISCOVER THE WORLD
OF THE QUEEN'S THIEF

✦ ✦ ✦

"I can steal anything."

New York Times–bestselling author Megan Whalen Turner's entrancing and award-winning Queen's Thief novels bring to life the world of the epics and feature one of the most charismatic and incorrigible characters of fiction, Eugenides the thief. The Queen's Thief novels are rich with political machinations and intrigue, divine intervention, battles lost and won, dangerous journeys, power, passion, and deception. . . .

"Unforgettable characters, plot twists that will make your head spin, a world rendered in elegant detail—you will fall in love with every page of these stories. Megan Whalen Turner writes vivid, immersive, heartbreaking fantasy that will leave you desperate to return to Attolia again and again."

—LEIGH BARDUGO,
#1 *NEW YORK TIMES*–BESTSELLING AUTHOR
OF *SIX OF CROWS* AND *CROOKED KINGDOM*

⎯⎯⎯⎯⎯⎯⎯THE THIEF⎯⎯⎯⎯⎯⎯⎯

Eugenides, the queen's thief, can steal anything—or so he says. When his boasting lands him in prison and the king's magus invites him on a quest to steal a legendary object, he's in no position to refuse. The magus thinks he has the right tool for the job, but Gen has plans of his own.

✦ ✦ ✦

"Trust me. Just read it. Then read it again, because it will not be the same river twice."—Lois McMaster Bujold

"To miss this thief's story would be a crime."
—*Bulletin of the Center for Children's Books* (STARRED REVIEW)

"A literary journey that enriches both its characters and readers before it is over."—*Kirkus Reviews* (starred review)

"A tantalizing, suspenseful, exceptionally clever novel."
—*The Horn Book* (STARRED REVIEW)

✦ ✦ ✦

A Newbery Honor Book

An ALA Notable Book

A YALSA Best Book for Young Adults

Horn Book Fanfare

A New York Public Library Book for the Teen Age

_____ THE QUEEN OF ATTOLIA _____

The brilliant thief Eugenides has visited the Queen of Attolia's palace one too many times, leaving small tokens and then departing unseen. When his final excursion does not go as planned, he is captured by the ruthless queen.

✦ ✦ ✦

"Megan Whalen Turner proves to be one of the brightest creative talents. With each book, she continues to add new levels and new lustre to her sparkling imagination."
—Lloyd Alexander

"Readers will be spellbound."
—*Kirkus Reviews* (STARRED REVIEW)

"Turner's storytelling is so sure that readers will want to go along with her—and discover whatever it is that Eugenides will do next."—*Publishers Weekly* (starred review)

"[An] intense read . . . thoroughly involving and wholly satisfying on all fronts."—*The Horn Book* (STARRED REVIEW)

✦ ✦ ✦

AN ALA*BOOKLIST* TOP 10 FANTASY BOOKS FOR YOUTH

ALA POPULAR PAPERBACKS FOR YOUNG ADULTS

A NEW YORK PUBLIC LIBRARY BOOK FOR THE TEEN AGE

PARENTS' CHOICE GOLD AWARD

———— THE KING OF ATTOLIA ————

Eugenides, no stranger to desperate circumstances, has gotten himself into difficulties he can't get out of. Used to being treated with a certain measure of wariness, if not respect, he suffers the pranks, insults, and intrigue of the court with dwindling patience. As usual, nothing is as it appears when he rescues a hot-headed young soldier in the Palace Guard.

"The King of Attolia is one of the most fascinating and original children's fantasies to have appeared in years."
—*The Horn Book* (STARRED REVIEW)

"A winner."—*Kirkus Reviews* (STARRED REVIEW)

"Eugenides, the former Thief of Eddis, is back and just as clever as ever."—*School Library Journal* (STARRED REVIEW)

A SCHOOL LIBRARY JOURNAL BEST BOOK

HORN BOOK FANFARE

ALA TOP 10 BEST BOOK FOR YOUNG ADULTS

NEW YORK PUBLIC LIBRARY BOOKS FOR THE TEEN AGE

———A CONSPIRACY OF KINGS———

When Sophos, heir to the throne of Sounis, disappears after an attempted assassination, those who care for him—including the thief Eugenides and the Queen of Eddis—are left to wonder where he has gone and if they will ever see him again.

✦ ✦ ✦

"Megan Whalen Turner is one of my all-time favorite writers. *A Conspiracy of Kings* is impossible to put down."
—Holly Black

"Turner's plotting remains deft, and the subtlety with which she balances her characters' inner and outer worlds will delight both series newcomers and fans."
—ALA *Booklist* (STARRED REVIEW)

"Unmissable."—*Kirkus Reviews* (STARRED REVIEW)

"Masterful."—*The Horn Book* (STARRED REVIEW)

✦ ✦ ✦

WINNER OF THE LA TIMES BOOK AWARD
A *NEW YORK TIMES* BESTSELLER
A BOSTON GLOBE–HORN BOOK HONOR BOOK
A *SCHOOL LIBRARY JOURNAL* BEST BOOK

_____THICK AS THIEVES_____

Pursued across rivers, wastelands, salt plains, snowcapped mountains, and storm-tossed seas, Kamet is dead set on regaining control of his future and protecting himself at any cost. Friendships—new and long-forgotten—beckon, lethal enemies circle, secrets accumulate, and the fragile hopes of the little kingdoms of Attolia, Eddis, and Sounis hang in the balance.

✦   ✦   ✦

"Immensely satisfying . . . this clever book is both a stand-alone introduction for those just discovering Turner's characters and a way to move the series forward to what promises to be a stirring conclusion for longtime fans. A must for fantasy readers."

—*School Library Journal* (STARRED REVIEW)

"Turner is a criminally underrated writer, and this standalone novel from her Queen's Thief series shows her again playing with narrative perspective, mixing history with fantasy to brilliant effect."—*Boston Globe*

✦   ✦   ✦

A *NEW YORK TIMES* BESTSELLER

HORN BOOK FANFARE

_____ RETURN OF THE THIEF _____

Neither accepted nor beloved, Eugenides is the reluctant linchpin of a truce on the Lesser Peninsula, where he has risen to be high king of the little kingdoms of Attolia, Eddis, and Sounis. As he struggles to keep his footing and counter the treacherous scheming of the Baron Erondites, Gen's impatient and unruly cousins threaten to revolt, and the ruthless Mede empire prepares to strike.

✦ ✦ ✦

"As readers bid farewell to this acclaimed series and its beloved cast of characters, it's clear that this concluding volume serves as the keystone, inextricably linking the preceding entries together in surprising yet inevitable ways; it's a bravura performance by one of our finest writers."

—*The Horn Book* (STARRED REVIEW)

"As intricately plotted as it is utterly satisfying, this series finale has everything readers could hope for from a conclusion twenty years in the making."

—*School Library Journal* (STARRED REVIEW)

✦ ✦ ✦

A *USA Today* BESTSELLER

The queen goes hunting.
The king sleeps in.
He stole my gold earrings
And left a stickpin!